PENGUIN CRIME FICTION

WICKED, LOVING MURDER

Orania Papazoglou, former Vassar student, bartender, and English professor, first introduced Patience C. McKenna in *Sweet, Savage Death* (also available from Penguin), which was nominated for an Edgar. She is at work on a third book for the series.

WICKED, LOVING MURDER

ORANIA PAPAZOGLOU

PENGUIN BOOKS

PENGUIN BOOKS
Viking Penguin Inc., 40 West 23rd Street,
New York, New York 10010, U.S.A.
Penguin Books Ltd, Harmondsworth,
Middlesex, England
Penguin Books Australia Ltd, Ringwood,
Victoria, Australia
Penguin Books Canada Limited, 2801 John Street,
Markham, Ontario, Canada L3R 1B4
Penguin Books (N.Z.) Ltd, 182–190 Wairau Road,
Auckland 10, New Zealand

First published in the United States of America by
Doubleday and Company, Inc., 1985
Published in Penguin Books 1986

Reprinted by arrangements with Doubleday and Company, Inc.

LIBRARY OF CONGRESS CATALOGING IN PUBLICATION DATA
Papazoglou, Orania, 1951–
Wicked, loving murder.
Reprint. Originally published: Garden City, N.Y.:
Published for the Crime Club by Doubleday, 1985.
I. Title.
PS3566.A613W5 1986 813'.54 85-31202
ISBN 0 14 00.8548 3

Printed in the United States of America by
George Banta Co., Inc., Harrisonburg, Virginia
Set in Electra

For Bill

WICKED, LOVING MURDER

ONE

Murder is only the beginning. No matter how final it seems when it happens—no matter how drastically you feel it's Changed Everything—for innocent bystanders, murder is only a prelude to a protracted bureaucratic nightmare that promises to outlast eternity.

I came to Writing Enterprises for the first time on the last day of the trial in what the newspapers insisted on calling the Agenworth case. It wasn't the Agenworth case. No one had ever been arrested for the murder of Myrra Agenworth, and no one ever would be. Myrra Agenworth's murderer had been arrested and tried and convicted of the murder of someone else. That was going to have to satisfy everyone.

I was due at Writing Enterprises at three-thirty, and I was late. I'd gone to Center Street to hear sentence pronounced. Myrra had been my friend. I had had something—some people said too much—to do with catching her murderer. I thought hearing sentence pronounced would be some kind of closure.

I was wrong. Maybe there is no closure in situations of this kind. Maybe there is, but I didn't want to find it. All I know is, going down to that courthouse accomplished exactly three things: it started the guilt machine working again; it allowed me to be cornered by newspaper reporters for the five millionth time; and it made me late at Writing Enterprises. The guilt was the worst of it, and the best. At that time of my life, I was hanging onto guilt like a sky diver hangs onto a parachute. Guilt made everything else possible.

Writing Enterprises was on the twentieth floor of an overly ornate pre–World War I building between Twentieth and

Twenty-first streets on Park Avenue South. The candy concession was run by an alcoholic who spent most of his time in the public phone booth on the other side of the lobby, talking to his bookie. The three self-service elevators never managed to be more than one third in service. It was a very bad building in a very good part of town. The owner had to be holed up in Jamaica somewhere, blissfully unaware that commercial rents in the Gramercy Park area were now well over thirty-five dollars a square foot.

The twentieth was the top floor. The elevator opened directly on the Writing Enterprises reception area. If I hadn't been so involved with my own problems, I might have noticed how seedy that reception area looked. The carpet was third-rate gray industrial broadloom, worn in the corners, stained near the edges of the receptionist's desk. The furniture was rickety and gouged, as if it had been picked up cheap at a bankrupt novelty company's distress sale. Either Alida Brookfield was working overtime to keep the decor of her headquarters in tune with the decor of the rest of the building, or Writing Enterprises wasn't doing as well as she said it was.

The idea that Writing Enterprises might be having financial trouble was so ludicrous I didn't even consider it. As I said, I was involved with my own problems. What do you do when the death of a friend leaves you so much better off than you'd been before she died that you don't want to go back? It had taken me a year to admit it, but once I had, I couldn't get it out of my head. *I didn't want to go back.* Before Myrra died, I was a magazine writer who did category romance novels on the side to pay the rent. I lived in a one-room third-floor walk-up on West Eighty-second Street. I took the subway everywhere, even at night. Now I had a book coming out from Doubleday, detailing my involvement in the Agenworth mess—a real book, with my name on the cover and my picture on the back flap. I had inherited Myrra's eleven-room apartment in the Braedenvoorst. I hadn't been on a subway for months. I missed Myrra, but I didn't want to go back to being who I was and what I was before she died. I couldn't convince myself that catching her murderer gave me the right to the things I had because she'd been murdered.

If that sounds irrational, so be it. That cold afternoon in February, I was feeling very irrational. I was also very preoccupied. If I hadn't been, the scene that erupted in the reception area would have made more of an impression on me.

It started with a woman with a face like a social worker's and a body like a piece of beef jerky. She came in just after I sat down, marched up to the receptionist's desk, and banged her fist on the carriage of the IBM Selectric II.

"I want to see Jack Brookfield," she said. "And I want to see him *now*."

The receptionist was a pimply, nervous girl named Janet. She had buck teeth, bitten-to-the-quick nails, and less than a high school education. Faced with what looked like the Wrath of God in the person of a dimly remembered maiden aunt, she fell back on formula.

"If you'll take a seat, I'll see if he's in," she said. She sounded like a B-movie actress impersonating a thirties telephone operator. The social worker wasn't having any.

"If he's not in, I'll wait," she said. "I'll wait if I have to wait a week."

Janet bit her lip. She looked from the social worker, to me, to the social worker again. Then she looked back at me and smiled.

"I'll see if Miss Brookfield's ready yet," she said. She got up, hurried into the corridor that started behind her desk, and disappeared.

The social worker turned her attention to me. She hadn't noticed me when she came in, which surprised me a little. I am six feet tall and weigh a hundred twenty-five. I have very long blond hair that falls to my waist. I am conspicuous at the best of times. That day I was wearing a long black skirt, black suede ankle boots, and a violently lavender sweater with leg warmers to match. I would have stood out at a convention of eccentrics.

The social worker didn't *see* me at all. She marched up to my chair, planted her feet wide apart and her hands on her hips, and stared at the wall just above my head. She was a small woman. If I'd been standing up, she'd have been looking at my chest.

"Do you have something to *do* with these people?" she asked me.

I rummaged in the pocket of my skirt for my cigarettes. For all I knew, she was one of those people who stand on street corners telling you the Russians have stolen their shoes.

"Don't have anything to do with Literary Services," she said. "Literary Services!" The expression on her face made it clear that, as far as she was concerned, she was uttering the Ultimate Obscenity. She looked down at the top of my head. "It's a racket," she said, a note of shrewdness creeping into her voice. "It's expensive, too. Literary Services—the only thing they service around here is their wallets, and they're not going to do it at the expense of mine."

I found a match and lit my cigarette, very slowly, very carefully. She still wasn't making much sense. I was no longer worried about her being a complete lunatic, but I did think she might be angry enough to be unreliable. Besides, I wanted to return to the always absorbing process of self-flagellation. I was comfortable there.

The social worker had no intention of letting me go. "Literary Services," she told me, "is where you send them a manuscript and they evaluate it. They're supposed to tell you how to make it *publishable*. They're supposed to tell you if it never will be publishable. They charge you a fee."

I coughed. It was a bogus cough, and we both knew it.

"They charge you a fee every time," the social worker said. "The same fee. I wrote a novel. That's a hundred and twenty-five dollars every time they read it. They read it six times."

This time my cough was real. I'd swallowed smoke. "Yes," I said, not knowing what else to say. "I've heard of things like that."

"Heard of them!" She seemed mortally offended that I'd heard of them. "I'll tell you what I think. I don't think they tell you how to make it publishable at all. I think they tell you things that won't make any difference, so they keep you coming back. If you did end up being published, you wouldn't be any use to them anymore."

I took a deep drag on my cigarette and decided not to say any more. I knew what she was talking about—I even knew she was right—but I didn't see what I could do about it that she wasn't already doing. "Literary services" *is* a racket. What you need when you finish a novel is an agent or a friend at a publishing house, not an evaluator.

As far as the social worker was concerned, what she needed was a lawyer. "I'm going to get them. I'm going to go to the Better Business Bureau, and I'm going to sue. Just you wait. By the time I'm finished with them—"

An overfed, overanxious young man with black hair just a little too long to be fashionable came chugging down the corridor, followed closely by Janet. His flesh was squeezed into a Brooks Brothers gray flannel two sizes too small for him. Perspiration had soaked through his jacket and made large dark semicircles under his arms. He held out his hands to the social worker.

"Mrs. Haskell!" He was working overtime to make himself sound exultantly pleased. "You should have called ahead! We could have had lunch!"

"I've had my lunch." She brushed by him without touching his hands. "I want to talk to you," she said, stalking into the corridor. "I'm going down to sit in your office and I'm not moving till I've had my say."

The young man frowned at her back. Then he adjusted his tie, straightened his back as if some mental nanny were reminding him of the benefits of Good Posture, and turned to me.

"You must be Miss McKenna," he said. "I'm Jack Brookfield."

I noted his age—no more than thirty-five—and decided he had to be Alida's son, not her husband. That was just as well. I had never heard of Alida having a husband.

"Patience Campbell McKenna," I said.

"We're all *thrilled* to have you here. We couldn't wait to see if you looked like—" He stopped. He had apparently decided that .

mentioning my newspaper photographs might not, under the circumstances, be a good idea. He cast a look over his shoulder, as if he expected to see an impression of Mrs. Haskell's back on the air in the corridor. "Amateurs," he said. "You don't know what a relief it's going to be to work with a real professional."

"I don't know if I want to be thought of as a relief," I said.

"Oh, it's a compliment, Miss McKenna, it's a compliment." He turned at the corridor and smiled at me, but he was already straightening his clothes and edging away. "I suppose I'd better go see to Mrs. Haskell. They get so overwrought, really. They don't *realize*—"

He whirled away again and plunged into the corridor. I put my cigarette out in the ashtray, half-smoked. I was just beginning to think I ought to spend some time considering the scene I'd just witnessed when a light went off on the phone on Janet's desk, and she stood up and smiled at me.

"That's Miss Brookfield now," she said. "You can go right in."

TWO

Writing Enterprises began as a single publication, *Writing Magazine*. I used to subscribe to it when I was at Emma Willard. I wanted to absorb a little of the atmosphere of the milieu, to feel like a writer while I was trying to become one. I failed. *Writing* was a stolid little how-to periodical concentrating on first-person technique, correct manuscript preparation, and admonitions to Write Only When Inspired.

Alida Brookfield changed all that. The old staff had been a superannuated Addams family whose religion was Literature.

Alida Brookfield was a businesswoman whose religion was fads. She imported Indian clothes when everyone wanted Indian clothes. She sold electric trains from a suffocatingly precious specialty store on East Fifty-fourth Street. She was even involved, once, with the manufacture of contraband hula hoops.

Writing promised to be more profitable than any of these. She bought it in 1972. In 1984, she still showed no inclination to move to another line of business. She had found her home.

Alida Brookfield was not worried about correct manuscript preparation, and she couldn't have cared less about inspiration. She changed the name of her newly acquired periodical to *Writing: The Magazine for Professional Freelancers* and concentrated on the financially exciting possibilities. There would always be people who couldn't write but wanted to be writers. There would always be people whose personal get-rich-quick fantasy was to produce the next sex-and-sin bestseller in their sleep. There would always be people who didn't know the score.

Her staff concentrated on the writing and selling of magazine articles—with the emphasis on "sell." Unwilling to thoroughly discourage their readers—thoroughly discouraged readers stop buying magazines—they concentrated on selling to magazines whose standards were low and whose rates of payment were even lower. MAKE BIG MONEY WRITING FOR THE SPECIALTY MAGAZINES, one cover promised. The author of that article was one Curt Hardy, whose credits included *Nebraska Heritage*, *The Antiquing Gazette*, and *Cat and Dog Times*. *Cat and Dog Times* pays a cent and a half a word. *Nebraska Heritage* pays half a cent. Since *Writing* couldn't ignore book publishing completely (too many people are working on epics about Bright Young Men Destroyed by Success), there was "Selling Your Novel," by Jean Pandric. Miss Pandric's new spy thriller had just been issued by Sparrowdale Press in Muncie, Indiana.

Laced through all this nonsense was some very bad advice. *Writing* was very militant about what it liked to call Writer's Rights. It urged its readers to Stand Up for Themselves with editors. If editors didn't like simultaneous submissions, that was just too bad. Magazine writing paid so little, writers couldn't afford *not* to make simultaneous submissions. If the editors of *Ladies' Home Journal* and *Good Housekeeping*, discovering you had submitted the same article to both of them at the same time, declared you'd never work for either of them again—they were just bluffing. If they weren't, you didn't need them anyway.

I have been in this business six years. I have been very lucky. My articles have appeared in most of the national women's magazines. My romance novels were issued by a major New York paperback house. Like most people in my position, *Writing* made me furious. The sight of it on a newsstand could paralyze me. The sight of it in one of my friend's living rooms could incite me to violence. I don't much like any of the writing magazines, but at least Miss Brookfield's competition, *The Writer* and *Writer's Digest*, made an effort to portray the business honestly. Alida Brookfield did not see the point in honesty. *Writing* earned its advertising revenue from vanity presses, make-a-thousand-dollars-a-week-in-your-spare-time schemes, and bogus literary agents based in Iowa. I once took a copy with a coverline on "How to Crack the Categories" and stuffed it down a lover's garbage disposal. I broke the garbage disposal. I didn't mind paying for it.

I did mind being in Alida Brookfield's office, but there was nothing I could do about it. Phoebe had blackmailed me into it. Phoebe could blackmail me into taking on the Iranian army if she went to work at it.

Alida Brookfield's office was a large corner room with a wall of windows looking up Park Avenue South to the Pan Am Building. What had been saved in the nondecoration of the reception area had been spent here. The hardwood floor had been sanded, polished, and covered with Persian throw rugs in reds and golds. The desk was a massive mahogany affair that looked more stable than the building. There was a wet bar in one corner. It opened on a glass-topped coffee table and a conversational grouping of plush-seated chairs.

Miss Brookfield rose as soon as I came in. It was like watching a wax dummy move. She was sixty-two, but she looked as if she'd been artificially preserved at the age of fifty. Her white hair was twisted into a French knot. Her green silk shirtwaist was straight from the third floor of Saks. Her nails were just round enough and just long enough and just palely colored enough for fashion. Her skin was plastic-smooth. She looked laminated.

She gestured with one hand at the conversational grouping and with the other at the two people standing to the left of her desk.

"Miss McKenna," she said. "How wonderful to see you here." She didn't smile. Her voice had no inflection.

The thin little man with the bald spot shifted from one foot to the other, looked at me, looked at the ceiling, looked at the floor, and then said,

"Maybe I ought to come back later. Maybe—"

Alida Brookfield tapped the top of her desk. The sound was louder than I would have expected.

"This is Mr. Lahler, our comptroller." She pointed at the thin man. "And this," she gestured to the young woman on Mr. Lahler's right, "is Felicity Aldershot, head of our Writing Workshops and Correspondence Schools Division."

Felicity Aldershot bore an uncanny resemblance to Glenda Jackson. She sounded like Glenda Jackson, too.

"We're so excited to have you here," she said, in a voice that owed something to the British midlands and something more to dramatic training. "We've all been so looking forward to this project."

Alida Brookfield began to lead the way to the conversational grouping. "We were discussing the consequences of last year's project," she said. "We expanded the Publishing Division, you know." She frowned. "You did realize we had a Publishing Division?"

I knew they had a Publishing Division. Writing Enterprises Books put out such titles as *Magazine Writing for Fun and Profit, Where Do You Get Your Ideas? A Sourcebook,* and *How to Make the Bestseller List Your First Time Out.* About two years ago, they had entered the category market. Writing Enterprises Books now published third-rate romances, fifth-rate westerns, tenth-rate mysteries, and unspeakable science fiction. At the back of each book was a ten-page essay on How to Write a (Whatever) by the author.

"We took our fiction list international eighteen months ago," Alida Brookfield said. "We're just now getting the returns. It was all dear Felicity's idea."

Felicity Aldershot nearly winced at the "dear." She overcame the impulse. She smiled instead.

"Miss Aldershot's from England," Alida Brookfield said. "She's been with us over eight years. She's made quite a difference to Writing Enterprises."

"Oh," Felicity Aldershot said. "Oh, no."

"It was her idea to take the magazine international," Alida said, as if stating something for the record. "The year after she came. Then Literary Services a year later. I had no idea how large a market there was in Europe."

Felicity Aldershot looked uncomfortable. Alida let her stay that way for a few seconds, then leaned back in her chair and sent both Felicity and Martin Lahler what my mother would call a Significant Look. Mr. Lahler started trotting toward the door.

Felicity Aldershot was more gracious. She smiled, said, "So nice to have met you" in an *Upstairs, Downstairs* voice, and made her way to the door with measured dignity. She closed the door with a sharp click. It was as if she'd run up a flag announcing that Miss Brookfield and I were now to be left alone.

Miss Brookfield offered me a pastel-papered cigarette from the gold cigarette box on the coffee table, took one herself, and sat down on one of the plush chairs.

"I suppose we ought to get right down to business," she said. When Alida Brookfield talked business, her voice sounded like tin. "We'd like to devote forty-eight pages of the July issue of *Writing* to an overview of the romance publishing business. Do you mind if I call it a business?" She looked as if she expected me to mind.

I shook my head. "It's all a business," I said. "Even literary publishing."

She was surprised and pleased. "That's fine, then," she said. "We try to treat it all as a business here. We try to teach our readers to approach writing and publishing as a business proposition subject to the rules and customs of business procedure." She wasn't saying anything, and she knew it. "For our romance section," she said, sounding very careful, as if she were considering this possibility for the first time, "we would like to include interviews with several successfully published romance writers. We'd like to talk to them about how they write what they write, why they write what they write, how they first broke into print—"

"Miss Brookfield." I reached into my pocket for my pack of Merits. Alida Brookfield's pastel-papered specials were the original coffin nails. They were strong enough to pierce wood.

"You talked all this over with Phoebe weeks ago," I said. "I know because it took her most of the last ten days to talk me into it. What it amounts to is this: you want to run sidebar interviews with Amelia Samson, Lydia Wentward, Phoebe Damereaux, Verna Train, Hazel Ganz, and Ivy Samuels Tree to accompany your special section articles. They will only agree to give these interviews if someone they trust edits the section. They want me."

"It's all perfectly ridiculous," Alida Brookfield said. "They have no reason not to trust my staff."

"They think they do."

"I don't have to agree to this, you know. Magazines don't usually allow interview subjects to look at their own interviews before publication. Never mind letting them hire someone to edit a lot of articles they had nothing to do with in the first place. I should throw you out of here."

"I wish you would."

"Why won't I?"

"The competition has already done articles on romance writing. *Writer's Digest* has done several. You weren't first so you have to be best, and to be best you've got to have those interviews. Besides," I said. "You'll put Phoebe on the cover and sell an extra fifty thousand on the newsstands."

Alida Brookfield sat back in her chair and crossed her legs. The silly part was over. "I keep trying to get Felicity to take over the magazine," she said, "but she doesn't want any part of it. Not that I blame her. We're giving people what they want, Miss McKenna. It may not be what you want, but it suits them just fine."

"My people want to be sure there are no inaccuracies in the articles. They don't want to see their faces plastered next to advice on phone queries."

"You make phone queries all the time."

"Only to editors I've worked with before. Worked with more than once."

"You don't understand what it's like for these people. They don't have the contacts you have. They're fighting for a chance."

"Phoebe spent five years in a fifth-floor walk-up on the Lower East Side, sending in stories over the transom. I came out after I left graduate school six years ago. I didn't have any contacts, either."

"These people live in places like Oklahoma. They can't all come to New York."

"Stephen King lives in Maine. It hasn't hurt him any."

"That's different."

I was about to tell her I knew why it was different, but I didn't see the point. The conversation was uncomfortable for both of us. Alida Brookfield wasn't used to defending herself. I wasn't used to arguing, for the sake of form, with someone who agreed with me but couldn't afford to admit it. I put my cigarette out in the blown-glass swan beside the gold cigarette box on the coffee table and said,

"As far as I can tell, this is the agreement. You have chosen the articles and assigned the writers for this section. These articles should have started to come in. Beginning Monday, I will come to the office every morning, like a regular employee. I will edit the articles, oversee the interviews of Miss Damereaux and company, pass on headlines and artwork, and do whatever else is necessary to ensure the section is something my people can live with. They will pay my salary, which has been negotiated at twenty-five cents a week. You will pay me nothing. Four weeks from Monday, I will disappear. We'll never have to speak to each other again. Unless we want to."

Alida Brookfield made a sour face. "Do you know anything about editing a magazine?"

"I was editor of a small national consumer monthly called *Fireman's Friend* for eighteen months. I hated it."

"This is a much larger operation."

"This is a forty-eight-page section."

"You can't expect us to change the fundamental editorial policies of this magazine for a small group of romance writers with prejudices that—"

I lit another cigarette, dropped it into the blown-glass swan, and put my head in my hands. "Miss Brookfield," I said, "it's been a long day. It's going to be a long night. I don't want to argue with you. I don't want to renegotiate the agreement. If you need something along those lines, talk to Phoebe. Just tell me one thing: yes or no?"

"Come with me," Alida Brookfield said. "I'll show you to your office."

THREE

My office was down three corridors, around four corners, and directly opposite the unpainted double doors of the Art Department.

The silly part wasn't over yet. Alida Brookfield wanted me to realize my exact position at Writing Enterprises. Since she owned

Writing Enterprises, she reserved the right to define that position. My office was a closet. Literally. Until a week before I entered it, the room had been respository for mops, brushes, and industrial-strength cleaner.

Offices were laid out along the corridors in descending size. Beginning with Alida Brookfield's Persian corner, the first main corridor contained (in order of diminishing importance) Felicity Aldershot's office (Writing Workshops and Correspondence Schools), Michael Brookfield's office (Newsletters), and Stephen Brookfield's office (Publishing). Jack's Literary Services started the slide around the corner and was the only office on that corridor with a person's name on the door. The other doors sported titles: Departments Editor, *Writing;* Domestic Sales, Publishing; Scheduling Coordinator, WWCS. The progression might or might not have had something to do with the importance of the positions in the firm. The progression on the first corridor, I was sure, had to do with nothing but Alida Brookfield's personal preferences in employees and relatives. Publishing—fourth on the list —had to be more important to the financial condition of the company than Newsletters, which was third.

My corridor contained Mr. Lahler, the Art Department, the men's and ladies' rooms, and me. The Art Department was one large room with rows of desks. Mr. Lahler's office was a cramped cubicle made more suffocatingly claustrophobic by being forced to accommodate two desks—a larger one for Mr. Lahler himself, and a smaller one for the timid little girl who was his assistant. Two plaques hung from the door. MARTIN LAHLER, COMPTROLLER, the first one read. The second said, ACCOUNTING DEPARTMENT.

Someone who looked like an emaciated Jack Brookfield was standing in Lahler's door when Alida and I came up to it.

"I don't want any arguments," he was saying. "For God's sake, Marty, it isn't a lot of money—"

Felicity Aldershot emerged from the Art Department, her hands in her hair. "Don't tell me you're fighting this out again," she said. "Alida made it absolutely clear—"

"I don't care who made what clear," the emaciated man said. "I've got a problem and I don't see—"

Jack Brookfield stuck his head out of the men's room. "It's *her* goddamn money," he said. "If she doesn't want you making an idiot of yourself in front of the entire population of Wall Street—"

"This has nothing to do with Wall Street."

"Commodities markets," Felicity Aldershot said. "That has to be the next step."

"My division is making a lot of money," the emaciated man said.

Felicity Aldershot gave him the fish eye. "Not that that has anything to do with you," she said.

At my side, Alida Brookfield decided the farce had gone far enough. She shuffled, coughed, and made a point of bumping into the pasteboard corridor wall. The little group around Lahler's office swung toward her immediately, straightening, as if they were drawing to attention. They were like a company in a forties army comedy, aware too late of the approach of their sergeant.

Alida Brookfield walked down the corridor ahead of me and stopped at Lahler's door. She looked the emaciated man up and down with palpable contempt.

"I don't care how much your division is making," she said. She turned to Lahler. "Everything I said stands," she told him. "I'm not putting any more cash into Steve's fliers, and I'm not putting up with Michael's—" She stopped herself. She had remembered my existence. "Never mind," she said. "You've got my instructions. All you have to do is carry them out."

"Someday somebody's going to carry them out on your head," Steve said. He gave Lahler a look of childishly impotent rage, one step away from plugging his thumbs in his ears and sticking out his tongue. Then he turned on his heel and strode off toward the more favored corridors. He looked right through me.

Alida Brookfield straightened her dress and her emotions and gave me a smile.

"Well," she said. "Miss McKenna. I'm afraid I haven't been able to give you a *large* office, but I've tried to give you a convenient one. You'll be able to see the mechanicals as soon as they come out of the Art Department."

Her expression said she was as likely to give a large office to someone in my position as she was to eat cow dung. I decided to ignore it. I'm not good at threats and counterthreats, and we'd had a long morning of those. I'm not good at handling myself in embarrassing situations, either, and no other situations seemed to exist at Writing Enterprises. Felicity Aldershot, Jack Brookfield, and Marty Lahler were frozen in the positions they'd assumed at Alida's entrance. They didn't look likely to move.

Alida put her hand on the knob of a door whose green BUILDING SUPPLIES sign had been inadequately concealed behind a sheet of white paper.

"We've put a desk in here for you," she said, swinging the door open and pulling a string to activate the overhead bulb. "And a coatrack and a phone. The phone's plugged into a jack in the Art Department, so be careful not to trip over the cord. We've even given you a closet."

She sounded so proud of the closet, I moved closer to look at it. It took up almost one entire wall of the minuscule rectangle I was supposed to live in for the next four weeks. It was an oversized portable wardrobe of peeling blond wood with mammoth double doors. I had a suspicion I would never be able to open those doors. If I tried, they would smash into the rickety little desk and office chair that had been crammed against the opposite wall.

"We can get you a typewriter," Alida Brookfield said. "If you think you'll need it." She obviously thought it would be beyond decency for me to need any such thing.

Felicity Aldershot was more accommodating. "Of course she'll need a typewriter," she said. "What if she has terrible handwriting? How will you read her memos?" She edged up to the door of the office and peered in. "There's an outlet in that corner," she said.

We all looked at the corner. Alida Brookfield considered the possibility that my handwriting might be too idiosyncratic to read.

"She can have Mary Lang's old typewriter," Felicity said. "Nobody's using it yet." I decided this was a euphemistic way of saying Mary Lang had quit—or been fired—but not replaced. I wondered what made Felicity feel the departure of an employee required euphemism.

Alida Brookfield looked around the office, frowning. "I suppose we could stock the closet," she said, sounding doubtful. "With paper and pens and things. So you wouldn't have to go running to the stock girl every time you needed something."

We all looked at the closet. I looked at the desk against the other wall. I decided it was a good time for pleasant accommodation.

"Well!" I said, actually making myself enter the room. The place made me feel as if I were choking. "This will do perfectly."

Neither Felicity Aldershot nor Alida Brookfield looked as if she believed me. I patted the top of the desk. I patted one of the doors of the wardrobe. I couldn't keep my hands off that wardrobe. It would have dwarfed a room three times the size of this one.

"I must admit it's a remarkably *large* closet," I said.

I *had* to find out whether those doors would open without demolishing the desk. I grabbed the knobs and pulled them toward me.

There was no place to go to get out of the way. When the body came tumbling out, it landed on top of me.

FOUR

Two things saved my sanity: the snow, and Detective Lieutenant Luis Martinez. The snow was the first of the Great February Blizzard, so named because it stopped traffic on the Fifty-ninth Street Bridge, shorted out three subway lines, and cut off all access to New Jersey within three hours of the first flake hitting the antenna on the Empire State Building. Lu Martinez was the man who had once arrested me for the murder of Myrra Agenworth.

I got Lu Martinez by the simple expedient of asking for him. I didn't bother to go through the usual rigmarole. I didn't report a homicide and request a certain detective be assigned to it. I just called One Police Plaza and asked for Lu Martinez. Then I went into a song and dance about what might or might not have happened to Michael Brookfield. Michael Brookfield was the body. I had managed to drag that much from a hysterical Felicity Aldershot and a livid Alida Brookfield.

Lu Martinez and I should not have been friends, but we were. He had arrested me. Before he arrested me, he harassed me. After I was no longer under arrest—because someone else was—he lectured me. None of it mattered. Lu Martinez spent a lot of his time on the Upper West Side and a lot of late nights in Original Ray's Pizza. I lived on the Upper West Side, couldn't cook, and was being nagged into a nervous breakdown by Phoebe, who thought I should gain weight. Lu Martinez thought I should gain weight, too. He bought large double-cheese-with-sausage pies and made me eat half of them.

I asked for him because I knew how he worked and because I knew I'd be doing him a favor. His Anita wouldn't marry him until he finished law school. He wanted to accumulate a year's vacation time, quit the department, and install himself full time at Brooklyn College. In order to accumulate a year's vacation time, he had to have excuses not to take vacations. I handed him one.

I was in the reception room when he came in, followed by the usual uniformed menagerie. I was on my fourth cigarette and my fifth prayer that a drink would miraculously appear from a mysteriously opening compartment in the gray industrial carpet. It didn't come from a compartment, but it came. Martinez had no sooner entered the reception area than he began rummaging in the pockets of his jacket. He'd gone through every one before he finally found the brass hip flask.

"Drambuie," he said, handing it to me. "I got it on the way over. The Drambuie, I mean. The flask was for a present. I was going to give it to you when your book came out."

Martinez couldn't wait for my book to come out. He was dying to see himself in print. He was desperate to know, as he put it, "what his character was like."

I took much too long a swig on the flask. Then I lit a cigarette and put the flask between my knees. The liquor calmed me just enough to let me feel sick.

The dead always void themselves. That was the first thing I thought of when the body fell on me. It was the only thing I could think of now. I thought of Julie Simms on the floor of my old apartment on West Eighty-second Street, of the blood seeping into the cracks in the floor and the smell of feces clogging the air. Trying to breathe near a newly dead body is like trying to breathe Jell-O. Rancid, moldy, soured Jell-O.

I took another swig from the flask. I was beginning to go hot and cold. I was beginning to go stupid. The uniformed men were running through the reception area, running through the corridor, running into the back offices. I could hear them shouting. Thirteen months ago, I wouldn't have known what was going on.

Up to then I had never read a murder mystery or a true crime book, never bothered with the crime articles in newspapers, never even watched police shows on television. Now I knew what they were going to do before they did it.

"You want to lie down somewhere?" Martinez asked.

I took another swig from the flask. Unadulterated Drambuie has remarkable medicinal qualities. Especially if you don't drink often.

"It fell on me," I said. "It *fell* on me."

"Jesus Christ."

"I should say *he* fell on me. Except I never knew him as a he. I only met him as an it."

"McKenna, for God's sake. You're getting hysterical."

"I'm already hysterical. Jesus Christ, Lu, it *fell* on me. It had that smell, that smell like Julie had, and then they—" I pointed at the corridor. *They* were barricaded in Alida Brookfield's office. Janet was guarding the back corridor, and the body. "You're not going to think I did you such a favor. You haven't met them."

"Keep me working and that's a favor."

"Somebody strangled him. With a typewriter ribbon. A silk typewriter ribbon. And they—" I gestured to the corridor again. I took another swig. I started yet another cigarette. Then I shook my head hard, as if physical violence were capable of clearing it. "Look," I said. "There he is, his eyes are coming out of his head, his skin is blue, in the name of God. Somebody stuffed him in that closet and there's that smell. And she—I mean, she's his mother or his aunt or something—she acts like he did it to her on purpose. She's furious with him. And she's—"

"McKenna."

"And then there's the other one," I said. "Felicity Aldershot."

"Felicity Aldershot?"

"I know, I know. Sounds like a romance writer. Sounds ludicrous. *Nobody* is named Felicity Aldershot." I stopped. That had triggered something, but between shock and Drambuie I couldn't figure out what. I brushed it off. "She's having a nervous breakdown," I said. "She's crying and carrying on. She vomits every thirty-three seconds. She keeps saying it's some woman—"

"Michael Brookfield was involved with some woman?"

"I don't know," I said. I explained the situation. Then I told him about the conversation in the hallway and the conversation since. My report about the conversation since was very sketchy. I hadn't been paying much attention. I hadn't been willing to hang around those people one minute longer than I had to.

"The general impression I get is he was involved with a lot of women," I said. "You can't really trust this, okay? I haven't been spending a lot of time *compos mentis* in the last hour."

"You haven't been spending a lot of time *compos mentis* in the last year," Martinez said. He bummed one of my cigarettes. He had a pack of unfiltered Camels in his pocket. Nobody can smoke unfiltered Camels forever. "I saw you at the sentencing," he said.

"I didn't see you," I said. I thought about the sentencing. "Didn't she look strange?" I asked him. "Strange and *off*, somehow. Crazy."

"She wasn't crazy. She didn't look any stranger than a lot of them look."

"I haven't seen a lot of them."

"You're about to see your second one." He sighed. "Take my advice," he said. "You look thin, you look ill, you look tired. You can't get yourself out of this, but you can minimize the damage. Go have Tony Marsh take your statement. Then get out of here."

"I'll only have to come back Monday," I said.

"Give it up," he said. "Give up the project. Phoebe will understand."

"She'll understand and she'll get screwed. Take a look around while you're here, Lu. They'll make her look like an idiot. They'll make them all look like idiots. They'll *lie*."

"They'll lie," Lu Martinez agreed, "and not just to their readers."

He sighed, stood, searched through his pockets again, and came up with the small bottle of Drambuie from which he'd filled the flask. "It wouldn't all fit," he said. "There's a little brass funnel thing on a chain around the flask neck. You fill it with that."

I took the bottle.

"Don't go see Tony Marsh," he said. "Stick around for the end. Go keep an eye on the menagerie."

FIVE

It was like walking into the cast of suspects scene in a really old Ellery Queen. Felicity Aldershot, Jack and Stephen Brookfield, and Martin Lahler took up the chairs in the conversational grouping. Alida Brookfield was seated behind her desk. They all looked up when I walked in. They looked away immediately.

There was a red leather wingback chair to the left of Alida's desk, with an ashtray on a stand beside it. I sat down and took out my cigarettes. I had the refilled hip flask in my bag. I left it there. I didn't want anyone asking for a snort.

The wet bar boasted forty-one different kinds of liquor. I counted them. No one else seemed to notice them.

I turned my eyes toward the window and watched the snow. It was already coming down fast and thick, blotting out the lights of the city in the distance. Snow is my favorite weather. It's quiet, beautiful, benign. In Weston, Connecticut, where I grew up, it almost always snows by the first of December.

"Love is a lot like snow," Nick told me once. "It's lovely to look at, but if you lie down and go to sleep in it, you freeze to death."

It was not one of our better weekends.

The snow, I decided, was making me think about Nick. I turned away from it and faced the conversational grouping. My relationship with Nick isn't bad, just draining. How draining may be inferred from the fact that I preferred to look at the tearful countenance of Felicity Aldershot than be reminded of the latest developments in the War of Commitment. Nick wanted a Commitment. I wanted a commitment without having to say I'd made a Commitment, which he didn't think was good enough.

Felicity Aldershot wanted an excuse to cry again. I tried to think of a way not to give it to her.

I needn't have worried. Felicity had no sooner put the sodden lump that had once been a white linen handkerchief to her eyes than Alida Brookfield rapped on the desk behind me. Every movement in the conversational grouping stopped dead. Felicity looked ready to swallow her tongue.

"What are they *doing* out there?" Alida said. "Why don't they come in and talk to us?"

They looked at me, suspicious, demanding. I was supposed to know something about these things. I had had experience. I couldn't deny it, either. A great deal of my experience had made the front page of the New York *Post*.

I gave the wet bar a hungry look and said, "They're photographing things. They—um—they'll probably have the body removed. The man from the medical examiner's office has to get here."

Alida tapped the desk again. "I don't see what all the fuss is about. He was strangled. Anyone with half a brain could see he was strangled."

"Shit," Stephen Brookfield said. "Remind me never to end up dead around this place."

"I've never been *quite* that lucky," Alida said.

"You just got luckier," Stephen said, trying to sound tough through the flush spreading over his face. "Now you don't have to figure out what to *do* about Mike's cooking his books—"

"Mike wasn't cooking his books!" Felicity Aldershot shouted.

Alida sat back in her chair. The chair was one of those executive swivel arrangements that threaten to tip over with any back-ward movement. Alida kept her balance perfectly. She folded her hands over her stomach.

"Of course Mike was cooking his books," she said. "Marty's known that for several months."

Marty Lahler looked pained. "It wasn't much of a recipe," he said. "It was just—" He stopped. He was trying to find the polite word. It wasn't possible. "He needed fifteen thousand dollars and he took it," he said finally. "He didn't even try to cover it up. Not really."

"Meaning he tried to cover it up, but he was bad at it," Alida said. "Par for the course."

"Even Mike could add." Felicity Aldershot was very angry. "And now he's dead and you're—"

"We're wasting our time," Stephen said. "Embezzlers kill ac-countants. Embezzlers kill heads of companies. People don't kill embezzlers."

"Somebody killed him," Felicity Aldershot said.

"So somebody killed him," Stephen said. "They didn't kill him for cooking his books. That wouldn't make any sense."

"You better hope not," Alida said.

Stephen got out of his chair, shoved his hands in his pockets, and walked to the window. The snow was coming down harder now. It was possible to see the other side of Park Avenue South. It was impossible to see farther.

Stephen found an unopened pack of cigarettes in his pocket and began fumbling with the wrapping. The pack was green. I'd never known a man who smoked menthols.

"You know," he said, "there are a lot of policemen out there. There's a spy in here." The others looked at me. "Instead of playing out the family psychosis, it might make sense if we tried to do something."

"We've already discussed doing something," Alida said. She blew smoke in my direction. "Before," she amended.

"Not the kind of doing something I meant," Stephen said.

"What do you suggest?" Alida was thoroughly exasperated.

She was making it clear. "Maybe we should launch our own investigation, catch Michael's murderer, and hand him over to the police."

"It wouldn't hurt."

"You've been reading detective stories."

"You haven't been." Stephen turned away from the window, went to the wet bar, and poured himself a drink. The rest of them reacted to that the way racehorses react to a starting bell. They rose in a body and attacked the liquor.

Stephen waited for them to get what they needed and sit down again. Jack had a small glass of milky green stuff that looked like crème de menthe on the rocks. Felicity Aldershot had a ten-ounce tumbler of straight gin. Marty Lahler had a Perrier and lime. He looked depressed.

Stephen leaned against the side of the wet bar and smiled benignly down at them. Stephen Brookfield smiling benignly had something in common with Dracula asking for an invitation to lunch.

"I don't think it would do us much good to find Michael's murderer," he said. "In case none of you realize it, one of us is Michael's murderer. One of us has to be."

"You're out of your mind," Felicity Aldershot said.

"One of us or Janet." Stephen considered. "I can't think of any reason for it to be Janet. Can you?"

"Maybe it was one of Michael's girls," Felicity Aldershot said. "Maybe she just walked in off the street. Anyone could have just walked in off the street."

"Janet would have seen him."

"Janet could have been away from her desk at the time."

"Whoever it was would have had to get out again. Janet would have seen him, then if not before."

"You don't know when any of this happened," Felicity said. "It could have been hours ago. He could have taken his time. He—"

Stephen Brookfield was shaking his head. He was also smiling again, but nobody wanted to look at his smile. He gestured at me with his glass.

"Ask our spy," he said. "He was still warm. He couldn't have been dead ten minutes when we found him."

Felicity Aldershot sank back into her chair. Jack Brookfield made a strangled sound, downed his crème de menthe, and headed to the bar for another one. Marty Lahler stood up and started pacing.

Only Alida didn't move. She was staring at Stephen. She looked venomous.

"You little bastard," she said. "You conniving, bloodless, predatory little bastard."

Her voice was perfectly emotionless. Even so, I was the only one who looked surprised when she picked up her marble-based appointment calendar and hurled it at Stephen's head.

SIX

Martinez got me out of there in time. I don't know what I would have done if he hadn't. I felt as if I ought to do something. If Alida had hit Stephen with that desk calendar, she would have killed him. She didn't hit him, of course. Her aim was execrable. I was still glad to see Officer Marsh stick his head through the door. If something hadn't stopped her, she would have gone on throwing things until she got what she wanted.

What she wanted was Stephen Brookfield, dead.

Officer Marsh looked even younger than the last time I'd seen him. An additional year on the police force had made him look more, not less, naive. He took me out the hall corridor to the reception area and deposited me on a chair.

"Lieutenant'll be right along," he said. He put his face close enough to mine to bite my nose and said, "Thought it was you. You don't have no luck no way, do you?"

I agreed with him and took out the hip flask. I was drinking from it when Martinez came to see me.

"Crazier than I thought," he said, dropping into the chair beside mine. He waved his blue stenographer's notebook in the air. "I shouldn't tell you what I've got till I get your statement," he said. "You want to hear it anyway?"

"You want to prejudice your case?" I asked him.

He shrugged. "Maybe you'll get another book out of it," he said. "You should be working on another book now, right? Before the last one comes out? So you won't get," he searched for the word, "spooked. By the reviews."

"Who've you been talking to?"

"Phoebe," he told me. "She's worried about you. I'm worried about you. That guy the lawyer is worried about you. You go around telling everybody you weigh one-twenty-five, but it ain't true, lady. You weighed one-twenty-five the first time I met you." He glossed over the first time he met me. "You're a *lot* skinnier than you were then," he said.

"Please," I said. "Don't try to feed me. Not now."

"I'm not trying to feed you," he said. "Drink the Drambuie. It's fattening. Phoebe says you go two-three days without eating anything sometimes."

"Not lately," I said. "Why don't you just tell me what you want to tell me."

"I want to tell you a couple of things. In the first place, I don't think you're going to be much of a noise on this one. You'll explain about finding the body, that will be it. Okay?"

"Okay," I said.

"Also, you're going to be here," he said. "You're going to be here for a legitimate outside reason, and I'm not idiot enough to think I'm going to talk you out of it. Not after the *last* time."

"So?"

"So you can help me out. You want to hear what I've got?"

I nodded. I really wanted to hear it, too. That was the other thing that got the guilt machine working. No matter what had happened or who it had happened to, I was capable of putting myself outside it and working it like a crossword puzzle. I *liked* working it like a crossword puzzle. When the crossword puzzle was solved, I wanted more crossword puzzles. It was not the sort of inclination I was brought up to think of as "decent."

Martinez was not worried about decency. It was his job to work crossword puzzles.

"It's the body that's got us all crazy," he said. "The ME's guy is pretty sure it was strangulation, but *that's* all right. Strangulation is strangulation. Thing is, the ME's guy thinks Mr. Brookfield was strangled in the closet. Not strangled and then shoved into the closet. Strangled *in* the closet."

"What the hell would he be doing *in* the closet?"

"How am I supposed to know?"

"You sure he wasn't pushed into the closet first, then strangled?"

"No," Martinez said, "I'm not sure. Nobody is sure. I'm just telling you what the guy thinks. He says first look shows no bruising, the way you'd have bruising if Brookfield had been shoved in. There's a frame around the doors. You'd have to step up to get yourself inside. You get shoved in, you bruise. No bruises." Martinez paused. "Could change with the autopsy," he said.

"But in the meantime, you want to know what he was doing standing in the closet. Because you think that's where he was."

"Right."

"Even if it sounds crazy."

"It fits," he said. "I don't know why it fits, but it fits. I can see it happening that way."

This was a side of Martinez I had never before suspected. It fascinated me.

"I always thought you were so rational," I said. "I thought it was Phoebe and I who were supposed to be the muddle-headed mystics. You and Nick were supposed to be rational."

He started to say something. I stopped him.

"Don't tell me you get an instinct for this sort of thing after a few years on the job," I told him. "I don't want to hear it."

"You don't have to hear it."

"What *do* I have to do?"

He stared at the ceiling. "I had a guy in the closet. I had a couple of guys going over the closet. I had a guy in the next room, in the accountant's office. You couldn't hear anything."

"No," I said. "Not through the pasteboard wall *and* the closet. I don't suppose you could."

"Don't know what anybody would want to eavesdrop on from there, anyway," Martinez said. "Lahler's assistant is a puffball. She hasn't got the intelligence to decipher a fifth-rate comic book. God only knows what Lahler talks to her about, but it sure isn't company policy."

"He talks to other people," I said.

"You think someone wanted to hear what he said to someone else? I mean, not to his assistant?"

"No," I said. "As far as I can tell from what's going on in there"— I jerked my head toward the corridor and Alida Brookfield's office —"everybody around here knows everything about everyone else anyway. Or practically everything."

"So what was he doing in the closet? In fact, what was he doing in that room? The place had been cleared out and set up for you. There wasn't anything in it anyone could want. Hell, there wasn't anything in it."

"Good point," I admitted.

"That's going to be your office," Martinez said. "You're going to spend a month in there." He looked at me sideways, trying to see if this upset me. It didn't. It *intrigued* me. Being intrigued made me guilty and anxious at once. I felt guilty for not being emotionally repulsed by the situation I was in. I was anxious that Alida Brookfield would use the death of Michael as an excuse either to change my office to another room or to call off the special section on romance writing and publishing altogether.

Martinez decided I was psychologically healthy. "Do you think you can keep an eye on that closet?" he asked me. "Without getting yourself killed?"

"Sure," I said. I was beginning to get a little drunk. I didn't care.

Martinez didn't care either. He took the flask from where I had left it between my knees and handed it to me.

"Have one more swig of this," he said. I did. He took the flask away and replaced the cap. "Weather's a bitch," he told me. "Go home and relax for the weekend. Drink a lot of tea. Eat too much."

"Right," I said.

"Stop off and have Tony take your statement first," he said.

"Right again." I dropped the flask into my bag. There was still a little liquor left in the Drambuie bottle, and I put that in my bag, too.

"Say hello for me to all the romance writers," he said. "I miss them."

A sudden vision of "all the romance writers" came through the mist of half-shock, half-alcohol that seemed to surround me. They were all out there somewhere, waiting for my report on the status of the special section. Once the news was out, they would want my report on more than that.

"I can see them now," I said. "A whole row of them. Lined up on my living room couch."

"You got a living room couch?"

"On my living room floor, then," I said, giving him a sour look. "Does it matter where they are?"

"It matters if you bought a living room couch." Martinez waved me away. "Go talk to Tony Marsh," he said. "I'll call you when we get the definite on the autopsy. I'll buy you a drink."

"Right," I said, thinking I'd been saying "right" a lot. I trudged around Janet's desk and into the corridor, uncomfortably aware that I was happier than I'd been for a long time. The only way it could go wrong, I thought, was if Martinez solved the thing before I managed to install myself at Writing Enterprises on Monday.

I tried to convince myself he wouldn't do something like that to me.

SEVEN

Martinez did not solve the murder over the weekend. Alida Brookfield did not move me to larger but less emotionally charged quarters, nor did she cancel the special section on romance. She never even considered canceling. When I finished making my statement to Tony Marsh, I found her waiting for me in the corridor. She was holding out a small pile of manilla envelopes.

"These are the articles that have come in," she said. "They'll give you something to do over the weekend."

I wanted to tell her I was going to have enough to do over the weekend. The first reporters had started showing up at the door. I could hear the whir of videotape machines in the reception area. We were going to make the six o'clock news.

Every romance writer from Gramercy Park to Los Angeles was going to know what happened at Writing Enterprises. Worse, they were going to know I was involved.

I took the envelopes, folded them under my pea coat, and made a head-down charge for the elevators. I was stopped four times. I had my picture taken two dozen times. Cornered by a frowning Chris Borgen with a WCBS microphone in his hand, I stuttered something about having been asked not to talk until the police made their statement (untrue) and escaped.

There was a foot of snow on the ground and a three-day traffic pileup in the street. A lot of people had abandoned their cars for the warmer, and more congenial, confines of Albert's and the Park Luncheonette. I could have asked for police escort home. Lu Martinez would have given it. I didn't want it. The Braedenvoorst was three and a half miles uptown, the wind was hitting me from both directions, the snow was coming down like hurricane rain—but I wanted to walk.

I walked into one of the most dismal weekends of my life. If there hadn't been thirteen inches of snow on Friday, nine inches on Saturday, and three and a half inches on Sunday, it would have been worse.

Romance writers are paranoids. They're paranoids with an excuse—God only knows they're made fun of at every possible opportunity—but the excuse makes their paranoia no less compelling. They *know* people are trying to make them look stupid. They *know* critics are lurking in broom closets, waiting for a chance to blame the decline of Western civilization and the erosion of world capitalism on the latest Silhouette Desire. They *know* there are traitors in their midst, spies, Quality Lit thugs who swoop into the world of love and lust to make a few thousand dollars under a pseudonym and then swoop out again, to surface in the pages of the *Village Voice* with articles accusing category romance of destroying the future of the women's movement. If they hadn't *known* all these things, I would never have ended up at Writing Enterprises.

Every paranoid needs a liaison to the rest of the world. The members of the American Writers of Romance had me. I was Phoebe (Weiss) Damereaux's ex-college roommate, best friend, and adopted pain in the ass. Phoebe was AWR president, also known as Queen of Hearts. Phoebe was one of their most successful and most visible members. Phoebe had appeared on the cover of *People*. Phoebe had talked for half an hour on Phil Donahue. Phoebe even had a book coming out *in hardcover*.

Getting a romance out in hardcover is next to impossible. Publishers hate romance even when they can relegate it to that intellectually invisible document shredder of literature, the paperback original. The AWR would do anything for Phoebe. If Phoebe said I was to be trusted, they would trust me.

They might have trusted me anyway. I am an ex-romance writer. I once wrote four books a year for Farret Paperback Originals. I wrote as Jeri Andrews and Andrea Nicholas (my brother has three children, Jeremy, Andrea, and Nicholas), but I hid only as much as I had to. I did, for instance, attend Myrra Agenworth's funeral. Myrra had helped over fifty women find work in romance, all of whom eventually went on to write Real Books or Real Magazine Articles under their own names. I was the only one who showed up to say good-bye.

Romance writers know what they're afraid of. For all the gushing nonsense they write on eternal love, for all the idiocies they blather on euphemized lust, there isn't one of them with a head softer than a rock. In the year before Writing Enterprises proposed their special section, articles had begun to appear touting romance as the easy way to break into publishing. Buy a phrase book, follow a formula, invest in a ream of heavyweight bond and six typewriter ribbons—and you can't fail. Anyone can do it. No talent necessary. No intelligence necessary. No contacts necessary. The lines will take *anything.* It drove every romance writer I knew crazy. It drove them doubly crazy because it wasn't true. It drove them crazy enough to try to take over Alida Brookfield's special section and use it for their own ends—a miracle I was supposed to effect with tact a career diplomat would have killed for.

I walked into my apartment to find six messages on my answering machine, a wicker basket full of glacéed fruit and Godiva raspberry crowns on my kitchen table, and a refrigerator full of Corning Ware casseroles. The food had undoubtedly been delivered by Phoebe, which meant that Phoebe was somewhere in the apartment. Where, I could only guess. Myrra had left me twelve rooms plus servant's wing. Phoebe could be anywhere.

The cat was standing guard at the refrigerator door. I got her a tiny saucer of Devon cream and a large bowl of 9-Lives Chicken & Cheese Dinner and sat down to listen to my messages. I had just made it through the third one—Amelia Samson, calling from the place she called The Castle, in Rhinebeck—when Phoebe came rushing into the kitchen.

"Turn that thing off," she said. "We're in a lot of trouble. We're in a *lot* of trouble."

Strictly speaking, *we* were in no trouble at all. I couldn't be arrested for the murder of Michael Brookfield because I had been in Alida Brookfield's office, or in the reception area in full view of one of three people, at the time it probably happened. Phoebe had spent the afternoon in a back room at the Fifth Avenue B. Dalton's, signing copies of *Flowers in the Storm*. Trouble came in the form of that premier example of the New Generation of Romance Writers, Ivy Samuels Tree.

Ivy Samuels Tree looked like one of those African statues meant to represent the queen of the Nile. She wasn't just beautiful, she was paralyzing. She could have stopped traffic in Herald Square at five minutes to nine on Christmas Eve. From her voice on the phone—the only contact we'd had until Phoebe got us all snowed in together that Friday—I'd expected the typical product of expensive boarding schools and repressive women's colleges in Massachusetts. I wasn't entirely disappointed. Ivy had gone to a very expensive boarding school—in Switzerland. She had even spent two years at Mount Holyoke. She had graduated, however, from the Massachusetts Institute of Technology. In theoretical mathematics.

"Your talent for mathematics stops when you start studying," she said, running a hand through her short Afro. "I started studying too early."

Phoebe put two casserole dishes on the table. One of them contained moussaka. Nick, who is Greek, taught us to pronounce the word "moos-sa-*ka*." The New York City habit of calling his favorite food "moo-*sak*-a" made him wild.

I was about to explain all this to Ivy—God only knows why—when Phoebe slapped a fork on the table in front of me and said, "This is all beside the *point*. Ivy's father was a scientist. Ivy was going to be a professor of mathematics. Ivy got married to a complete idiot instead. It's all ancient *history*, for God's sake."

"What are we supposed to talk about?" I said. "You come here, you fill my apartment with a lot of strange food, you sit me down with someone I've never even met—what are we supposed to talk about?"

"Today." Phoebe deposited herself demurely in her seat beside the casseroles. "You're supposed to talk about what happened today."

"What happened today?"

Ivy gave me a very weak smile. "I was there," she said. "In that guy's office. The one who got murdered."

I pushed away the plate of moussaka Phoebe offered me and opted for a cigarette instead. "When?" I said.

"Must have been quarter to four," Ivy said.

"Oh, for God's *sake*."

Phoebe got to her feet and started pacing, throwing her hands in the air. "Don't *get* like that," she said. "This is serious."

"I know it's serious," I said. "Quarter to four." I turned to Ivy. "You had to be there within fifteen minutes of when he was murdered. It was about quarter after when we found him. What were you doing there?"

Ivy hesitated, then reached into the large carryall she'd left on the floor beside her chair. She came up with a thick paperback. She handed it to me. "Look at that," she said.

I looked. It was a copy of *Queen's Gambit*, a romance novel that had been making quite a showing on the racks for the past few months. Inscribed under the title, in flowing script, were the words, "by Ivy Samuels Tree."

"Turn it over," Ivy said.

I turned it over. On the back were an author bio and a picture. The bio was authentic. The picture was of a blowsy, forty-year-old bleached blonde.

"My alter ego," Ivy said.

"Which is supposed to mean what?" I asked her.

"Which is supposed to mean romance writers can't be black," Ivy said. "Black romance writers don't sell romance books."

EIGHT

It was worse than it looked in the beginning.

"It's written into my contract," Ivy said. "I'm not supposed to let anyone know. I'm not supposed to appear anywhere as Ivy Samuels Tree. I'm not supposed to give interviews except over the phone. I've been calling myself Ivy Samuels again since the divorce, so that's no problem, but lately—"

"Lately she's wanted to change the terms of the agreement," Phoebe said. Then she gave me one of her Very Significant Looks. "It's an exclusivity contract," she said.

"They've got a clause in there that says they can suspend everything—not pay me any royalties, even if they owe them to me, not publish any of my new books—if I do anything that might, and I quote, 'possibly prejudice sales potential.' They can suspend me and not get rid of me, if you see what I mean."

I saw what she meant. If Ivy's publishers, Dortman and Hodges, "suspended" her contract, Ivy would not only not make any money for her work for them, she'd be unable to sell her work anywhere else. No other publishing company would want to take a chance on being sued by Dortman and Hodges for violation of Ivy's exclusivity clause.

I lit another cigarette and considered the situation. "None of this would hold up in court, would it? I mean, once you got it across that it was your being black that bothered Dortman and Hodges, then it would be discrimination, right?"

"Right," Ivy said. "I've been talking to Phoebe's lawyer friend about it."

Phoebe gave me a dirty look. Her lawyer friend is my Commitment friend, Nick. Phoebe thinks I am Treating Nick Badly.

"The problem," Phoebe said, "is time."

"Five years of time," Ivy agreed. "That's how long Mr. Carras thinks it would take before all the appeals were through and everything was clear. We decided not to fight it head on. There are other ways. And I can't afford to go five years without making any money."

My head was beginning to hurt. "Jesus Christ," I said. "Whatever possessed you to sign a contract like that? You're an educated woman."

"At the time I was an educated woman with two children, no job, no husband, and a dollar fifty-three in the bank."

"Right," I said.

"I couldn't go to my father, either," Ivy said. "I married the original black-power militant. My father was a self-made man who thought *being* self-made was the only thing anyone had the right to be proud of. My father didn't speak a word to me from the day I married John Tree till the day the divorce became final."

"You signed the contract before the divorce became final."

"I had to."

"Right," I said again.

Phoebe tugged at my sleeve. "I think we'd better get to today," she said. "I mean, now that you have the background." She pushed her plate of moussaka away, for once not particularly worried that all the food she'd made was getting cold. "It's this Michael Brookfield person who's important."

I thought about Michael Brookfield with a typewriter ribbon around his neck and got up to get the Scotch and the Drambuie from the cupboard. When I put the bottles on the table in front of Ivy, she looked ready to canonize me.

"Michael Brookfield wrote me a letter," Ivy said. I passed out glasses. "He runs this newsletter," she started again. "I guess he runs a lot of them. One on each of the genres—westerns, science fiction, mysteries, and romance. Soft core porn, maybe. Anyway, the newsletters have a lot of different sections to them. Mostly it's how-to columns and market information, but there's always a sort of gossip part, with little items on people in the field. Brookfield's letter said he had a picture of me, and the whole story of the contract, and he'd heard I was seeing a lawyer, and he was going to write a column on what a terrible thing had been done to me. It all sounded very sympathetic."

"Sounded?"

Ivy slugged back most of her glass of Scotch. "I don't think you write a letter like that," she said. "You just go ahead and publish the column. You don't write a letter like that to tell someone you're writing a column."

"You mean he was trying to blackmail you," I said. The idea had possibilities. Michael Brookfield had had "women."

"I made an appointment," Ivy said. "I got there around quarter to four. I got shown right in. God, he was a weird little man. He kept going on and on about the indignities I'd suffered. Why in the name of Christ do white people go on and on about the indignities I've suffered? Worst indignities I've ever suffered have been being forced to listen to white people tell me what indignities I've suffered."

I poured her another glass of Scotch. I poured myself a glass of Drambuie. Phoebe considered Ivy's last speech, decided she knew which way the evening was going, and went to get herself a bottle of André pink champagne from the refrigerator.

"John Tree used to give me a lot of shit about the indignities he suffered," Ivy said. "I used to kick his ass. I hate people who *define* themselves as basket cases."

"What do they teach you in those boarding schools?" Phoebe said. "Every woman I know who went to a boarding school swears her head off."

Ivy and I said, "Wouldn't be surprised," simultaneously. Then Ivy knocked back her Scotch and poured herself another one.

"I wasn't going to pay anyone blackmail," she said, "and I wasn't going to let myself get kicked around. I went into this man's office in a very belligerent mood. Well, I never got a chance to say anything. He talked nonstop for about five minutes and didn't make any sense at all. Then he got a phone call."

"Interoffice or outside?" I asked her.

"Couldn't tell," she said. "Whoever was on the other end did a lot of talking. He did a little squeaking. Then he put the phone down and said he had to go down the hall for a minute. Then he disappeared." She stared at the Scotch bottle. "He looked green," she said finally. "I mean he actually turned the color green. He had really pasty, unhealthy looking skin, alcoholic's skin, and it just turned a different color."

I put a very considered amount of Drambuie in my glass. The way the day had been going, I was getting pretty woozy. I didn't want to miss anything.

"Did he come back?" I asked Ivy.

"He came back," she said, "but I better tell you what I did before he came back. I went through the papers on his desk."

"What?"

"I went through the papers on his desk," she repeated. Then she shrugged. "It seemed like a good idea at the time," she said.

"What could he possibly have had on his desk?"

"What didn't he have on his desk," Ivy said. "He's supposed to be putting out newsletters. He's got old copies of *Vogue*. He's got three pictures of some woman, stark naked yet, lying on a bearskin rug. He's got a financial report on Writing Enterprises. He's got cover proofs for four or five paperback books—two-color covers, really garish. He's got a couple of textbooks stamped 'Harvard Business School' and inscribed to somebody with a Polish name. He's got a whole bunch of letters written on the letterhead of a stock brokerage to someone named *Jack* Brookfield. It was crazy."

"Letters from a stockbroker?" I said. "To *Jack* Brookfield? Are you sure it wasn't Stephen?"

"It was Jack."

"Do you remember the firm?"

"Not one of the big commercials," Ivy said. "I might remember it if I heard it again. Anyway, I heard a noise in the hall and went back to my chair. A couple of seconds later, he walks in, looking greener than when he left. He doesn't even sit down. He sticks out his hand, says nice to have met you, but something's come up and can we talk another time. He got me out of that office and into the elevator in thirty seconds flat."

I thought of the reception area, the carpet, the elevators. "Was Janet at her desk?" I asked. "The receptionist?"

"Nobody was at the desk."

"Did you pass someone in the hall?"

"Nobody saw me leave, if that's what you mean."

"I suppose somebody saw you come in," I sighed.

"Somebody *was* at the desk then."

"It figures."

"Just one more thing," Ivy said. "I looked at the wall clock when I got into the elevator. It said five after four."

NINE

We should have called Nick—or even Martinez—and put the whole mess in official hands. Janet would remember Ivy Samuels Tree. A blind-drunk psychotic would have remembered Ivy Samuels Tree, and Janet looked like neither a drunk nor a mental defective. One of the things I learned after Myrra was murdered was that, if there is no way out, the best course of action is to find a way further in.

We finished the liquor instead. We were in no shape to cope with common sense. Martinez was lost in the snow and Nick—according to my answering machine—was at the Knicks game. Nick always calls on Friday to leave his weekend schedule. He calls on Monday to give me the details of basketball games, football games, ice hockey games, baseball games, and nights on the town with his new partner, David Grossman. Nick wants to let me know that, although he refuses to sleep with me, he isn't sleeping with anyone else.

At four o'clock in the morning, I got out the sleeping bags. I have six bedrooms but only one bed. I have five common rooms but only one table and four chairs. I write in the kitchen. What Myrra actually left me was the apartment and everything in it at the time of her death. Everything in it, with the exception of the five-by-three-and-a-half oil portrait of Myrra herself, had gone to Sotheby's for auction. The auction money paid the maintenance on the apartment. It could have paid for much more, but I didn't want to touch the money. I didn't want to buy furniture, either.

Ivy was too polite to comment on the emptiness. Phoebe had lectured me too often to want to take it up again after all that champagne. They took two of my sleeping bags to separate rooms in the back hall and set themselves up in splendor on the floors.

The snow was still coming down at noon Saturday, when we woke up. Hunan West was delivering anyway. We ordered fifty dollars worth of Chinese food and stayed in to nurse our hangovers. While we were asleep Nick called my answering machine again—to tell me he was going shopping and then straight to a Rangers game.

When Martinez called me Sunday afternoon we still hadn't reached Nick. We had come to exactly one decision. Considering how Nick felt about murder suspects, even possible murder suspects, talking to the police without presence of counsel, we would not say anything about Ivy to Martinez until we tracked Nick down.

Martinez met me in the Copper Hatch at nine. I turned down Drambuie for Perrier and pie. Martinez looked at my eyes and tutted.

"Rest," he said. "I told you to get some rest."

"All I did yesterday was sleep," I said.

"All you did Friday was drink."

"I had help," I said. I saw how interested he was and shook my head. "Phoebe," I told him. "Nick was at the basketball game."

"Why that guy doesn't dump you is beyond me."

"It's beyond me, too," I said. "I know why I don't dump *him*. He's six eight and he looks like Christopher Reeve."

"He's a good man."

I must have started to look stubborn. Martinez dropped the subject. He pulled a large white business envelope from his jacket pocket and threw it on the table next to my pie.

"Medical report, lab reports, vet on Brookfield," he said.

"You're crazy," I said. "You're going to get fired."

"I'm quitting anyway. You're writing another book."

"Not yet I'm not."

"Take a *look* at it."

I pushed the envelope away. I was feeling more than a little guilty about Ivy Samuels Tree, still camped out in my apartment. I also didn't want to break the regulations of the New York City Police Department.

"Why don't you just tell me," I said. "It'll save time that way. We came here to talk, after all."

"Keep the envelope," he said. "You'll need it later."

I hesitated. Then I picked it up and stuffed it in my bag. Martinez was right. I might need it later. If I intended to go on writing true crime, Michael Brookfield's murder was an opportunity I wasn't going to be able to turn down. Besides, Martinez knew me. If I refused that envelope, he'd get suspicious.

"Medical report's got no surprises," he said. "No bruises, by the way. No bruises at all, which they tell me is very unusual. Nothing to say he got pushed into that closet. Doesn't make any sense he'd have got into the closet without being pushed, but you never know."

"He was strangled?" I asked.

"Definitely strangled. Almost definitely with that typewriter ribbon we found around his neck. Strangled, by the way, not much before you found him. Hour at most. If you can trust the statements we got out of that crew, and I don't think you can, half an hour at most."

"They saw him?"

"Everybody saw him. Everybody saw so much of him, you'd think nobody had time to do him in."

I winced. Martinez didn't notice.

"No big deal with the lab report," he said. "Place used to be a broom closet or something. Half a dozen sets of prints but they don't mean anything. The vet, however, has a few interesting points. You ready?"

I nodded.

"First place, not women but woman. One. Your Miss Brookfield might have thought there were more, but there was just the one. We could turn up something later, but I don't think we will. He'd been seeing her for five years and he'd been spending a lot of money on her. She likes to travel. He took her to Greece and Italy five or six times a year. He took her to Switzerland last summer. We got his credit card records from his apartment. You should see his apartment."

"Fancy?"

"Impoverished. It made that dump you were living in on West Eighty-second Street look good. Furniture straight out of the Salvation Army. Carpet a hundred years old. Pullman kitchen. You want to know what he took home working at Writing Enterprises? Fifteen thou a year."

"Nobody can live in Manhattan on fifteen thou a year."

"Nobody can take women summer skiing in Switzerland on fifteen thou a year, that I know. The apartment was down on Avenue A. Brookfield had this arrangement with Alida Brookfield. She paid rent on the apartment and his bills at Brooks Brothers. Otherwise he was supposed to be living on his salary."

"I told you they thought he was cooking the books," I said.

"We're checking it out," Martinez said. "But he had to be, McKenna. There's no other explanation for it. Not unless he was running drugs on the side—and before you start, I checked. If he'd been any kind of operator, somebody would have heard of him. Nobody's heard of him."

"Okay," I said. "So he's been cooking the books." He might also have been blackmailing people, but I couldn't say anything about that without giving Ivy away. Besides, even Ivy didn't really know if he'd intended to try blackmail. The conversation had never got that far.

"He had all these wonderful reasons for murdering people," I said. "Nobody seems to have had a reason to murder *him.*"

"Yeah," Martinez said. He called the waitress and ordered me another piece of pie. He ordered a Jack Daniels for himself. "Trouble is," he said, "somebody told me that bunch'd murdered someone for kicks, I'd believe him."

"Me too," I said.

"They're her nephews, by the way," he said. I looked blank. He explained. "Alida Brookfield. The boys are her nephews, not her sons. According to Miss Brookfield, she's never been married."

I almost explained a few things to him. Like where babies come from.

TEN

Alida Brookfield's driving passion was her need to destroy the egos of her relatives, her friends, her subordinates, and her employees. When I got to Writing Enterprises Monday, she was working on poor, fat Jack. I always thought of him as poor, fat Jack. He never stopped trying too hard to please.

"It's not enough I've got the other two," she was screaming as I came off the elevator. "It's not enough I've got the police occupying these offices the way a conquering army occupies a defeated country. You've got to drag your vicious, deceitful, ungrateful, *stupid*, excessive—what do you think I work for? What do any of you think I work for?"

The screeching was replaced by a low murmur. I shifted the newspapers under my arms and made a face at Janet.

"She ought to shut the door." I gestured at the corridor.

"She *did* shut the door." Janet stared at my newspapers. She started to say something, thought better of it, and went back to her typing.

"You'll put it back," Alida Brookfield shouted. "You'll put every last cent of it back. You'll put it back by Friday. Do you hear me, Jack? By *Friday.*"

I considered sitting down in the reception area and reading the papers there. I didn't want to find myself outside Alida's office as Jack came hurtling through the door. I didn't want to be seen in the hall while she was still screeching. The last thing I needed was the staff of Writing Enterprises conscious I had once again Heard Everything.

"I don't understand what's wrong with you people," Alida screamed. "You were all gassed at birth, I swear to God. The shit that goes on around here—don't think I don't know what goes on around here. I give you a simple assignment, I give you directions, you can't even follow directions. You're bad, Michael was worse, and Stephen is the worst of the three of you. You can't do your work, you can't save your money, you haven't got sense enough to know truth from fraud—"

I sighed and started into the corridor. I couldn't read the papers in the reception area. The *Post* headline read LOVE GIRL IN NEW MURDER PROBE. The *Daily News* had my picture on the cover. Only the *Times* managed restraint. Michael Brookfield's murder having made the lower left corner of the front page on Saturday, the *Times* saw no further need to shout. The story had been relegated to the second, otherwise known as the Metropolitan, section.

With one thing and another, I had never seen the Sunday papers. I was beginning to think it was just as well.

There was the sound of glass breaking against a wall. I jumped, stared guiltily at Janet, and hurried into the corridor. I couldn't stand around all day, framed by blowup posters of *Writing* magazine's most famous covers. GETTING THE MOST FROM THE LEAST, one cover said. "How to cut down on time—and energy—and still sell the articles you write!"

I knew a perfect way to save time and energy. All I had to do was catch a cab to Grand Central and a New Haven line train from there to Danbury. My brother would pick me up and take me home. Martinez wouldn't even mind. He knew me well enough to realize I'd come back if he needed me.

I was halfway down the corridor, doing my best to stride purposefully, when I first heard Jack.

"You know who it was, you bitch!" he yelled. "You know who it was and so do I."

"I know who does your work," Alida yelled back. "I know who does it and why you can spend all your time in the men's room. What do you think I am, blind? I know everything that goes on around here. I've always known. You don't fool me for a minute—"

Felicity Aldershot was standing just outside Alida's door. Her head was cocked. Her hands were full of outsized sheets of yellow, orange, and light blue printed paper. She looked up when she saw me and gestured helplessly in the direction of the argument.

"Do they do this often?" I asked her.

"Alida isn't very good with people," she said.

"What are those?" I pointed at the colored papers.

She looked down at the stack in her hand, as if she'd forgotten they were there. Then she straightened them. She needed something to do with her hands.

"Newsletters," she said. "Yellow for mysteries, orange for westerns, blue for science fiction. The romance newsletter is pink, but that was in Michael's office, and the police have that sealed."

I was surprised. Someone once stabbed a woman nine times in my apartment on West Eighty-second Street. It had taken exactly forty-eight hours before the seal was off.

"Are they in my office, too?" I asked her. I couldn't do anything about the wardrobe if I couldn't get into the office. Martinez might have left word with whoever was on duty to let me in if I asked. If he had, he'd been stupid. He wasn't usually. I wouldn't go near the place under those circumstances.

Felicity Aldershot was shaking her head. "No, no," she said. "*Your* office is okay. It's Michael's and Marty Lahler's they've got locked. Though I can't see what they want—" She stopped, took another look at Alida's door, and shrugged. "The work has to go on," she said. "Just because someone's died, no matter how tragically, doesn't mean the work doesn't have to be done."

"Right," I said. I didn't know if she was right or not. I didn't even care.

There was another round of breaking glass. Alida Brookfield said, "I don't care who did what. All I want is you to fix it."

Felicity Aldershot winced. "She doesn't realize. You have to work *with* people's shortcomings, not against them."

"Why does she keep them around? If she doesn't think they do a good job?"

"Family," Felicity Aldershot said expressively. She cast her eyes to the ceiling, like a maiden in a Victorian melodrama. "She has very *American* ideas of family."

"You're all bastards," Alida Brookfield said. She sounded like she meant it.

I decided to leave Felicity's definition of "American ideas of family" alone.

"When she's through with the family," I said, "could you ask her to come along and see me? I read the articles she gave me."

Felicity's face cleared. Her mouth arranged itself in a Howard Johnson hostess smile.

"I can help you with those," she said. "I have everything in my office."

ELEVEN

"*I have everything in my office*," Felicity said. She might have meant that literally. There was a workshop chart on the left wall near the windows, but it was the only sign of Felicity's assigned responsibility at Writing Enterprises. The rest of the office was crammed with other people's work—Michael's newsletters, Jack's evaluated manuscripts, Stephen's category line tip sheets. Alida was supposed to be editor-in-chief of *Writing* magazine, but the plans for the special romance section and the inventory card-file were in Felicity's office.

"When do you have time to run correspondence courses?" I asked her.

She laughed. "Running correspondence courses doesn't take any time," she said. "We job out to freelancers mostly. It's cheaper. It saves office space and they pay their own social security. The conferences are a little more work, but less than you'd think. And that's only four times a year."

"You still have to hire a hall," I said. "And then there's the schedule, and the food, and the speakers—"

"We get the speakers from our own stable," Felicity said. "They're not a problem, really. Most of them need the work and the money, so they don't let us down too often. Special speakers are something else, of course, but there are never more than one or two of those."

"And the hall? And the food?"

"I made special arrangements with the hotels five years ago. They still stand. I made out a master conference schedule eight years ago. I've never had to change it. It's all very simple if you're efficient."

I knew computers that weren't that efficient, but I didn't mention it. I dumped the newspapers on Felicity's well-carpeted floor —three-inch pile, in mauve—and began to rummage in my bag for the articles. They were still in their manilla envelopes. I threw them on Felicity's desk.

"These are impossible," I said. "Even she must know these are impossible." I jerked my head toward the left wall, beyond which the fight of the century had diminished to a low angry hum, like the sound near telephone poles on hot summer days in the country. "I've only read them once, but I don't even think they're salvageable."

Felicity Aldershot sat back in her chair and smiled. She was playing the Wise Parent Gently Exposing the Muddled Thinking of an Impressionable Child. Her desk was a modern sculpture in mahogany. The prism on the blotter was from Steuben Glass. Her office was smaller than Alida's but it had cost just as much to furnish, if not more.

She tapped the envelopes. "What do you think would make

them *salvageable?*" She made the word sound like something in a foreign language.

"Look," I said. "There's this thing by Ronald Harbank." I looked through the envelopes and found it. " 'Writing the Romance—A Surefire Recipe.' In the first place, I don't think Ronald Harbank has written a romance. He's never written one I've ever heard of, anyway, and I hear of a lot of them. And if he was anybody in the field, I would have met him." That was true enough. Phoebe, like Myrra before her, "took up" new romance writers. Her parties were populated by the oddest people.

"Mr. Harbank writes as Jessica Henry for Zedidiah," Felicity said.

I made a face. "Zedidiah is a tenth-rate house with a nasty reputation," I said. "They operate almost entirely work-for-hire. Never mind the fact that they've got zero distribution."

"Now, now," Felicity said. "Everybody can't write for the major houses, you know. Zedidiah gives a lot of unknowns a chance."

"Zedidiah gives a lot of unknowns the shaft," I said. "Acme would be bad enough, for God's sake, but at least they put out a halfway decent romance line. Zedidiah buys and publishes crap."

"Zedidiah buys and publishes manuscripts they receive over the transom," Felicity Aldershot said. "The purpose of *Writing* magazine is to help our readers get published. Don't be fooled by the subtitle. We call it *The Magazine for Professional Freelancers*, but our major audience is the unpublished writer. Zedidiah will give that writer a chance."

"I'll repeat myself," I said. "Zedidiah will give that writer the shaft. Any of the lines will buy manuscripts over the transom, even the ones that say they won't. And the agents are happy to see new work. A successful romance writer can make them a lot of money."

"The major lines buy one manuscript over the transom for every two thousand they reject," Felicity Aldershot said. "Those odds are close to impossible."

"Those odds are the best in the business."

"*If* you stick with the majors," Felicity said. "Most of our readers would be overjoyed to come out with a small press. Besides, if they publish a book with a small press it may give them a chance to publish something with a larger press, next time."

There was an ashtray on Felicity Aldershot's desk, half-concealed by a pile of reports on the story preferences of science fiction readers. I pulled it into the open and lit a cigarette over it. The problem was not in what Felicity was saying, but what she wasn't saying. She wasn't saying it depended on which small press. She wasn't saying it depended on how good the book was to begin with. She wasn't saying that Mr. Harbank's article made all these conjectures superfluous.

I flipped the article open to the middle. "Do you realize what he's advocating here?" I asked her.

"He's advocating science," Felicity Aldershot said smoothly. "This is a very scientific method."

"He's advocating plagiarism," I said. "For God's sake, Felicity. Maybe it's not plagiarism in the legal sense, but it's plagiarism any other way. First you're supposed to read ten romance books. Then you're supposed to go through them with a lot of felt pens. You underline dialogue in red. You underline description in yellow, you underline action in green. You figure out how many pages there are to an average chapter. Then you use this—this color scheme—like a blueprint and write in words that fit."

"So?"

"So you don't write your own book," I said. "How do you expect them to move from a smaller press to a larger press when all they're doing is using other people's ideas, other people's structures, other people's methods? How do you expect them to produce anything original?"

Felicity Aldershot said, "I don't."

It was a standoff. We were not coming from two competing but complementary points of view. We were not speaking the same language in the same universe. Felicity Andershot did not want to help the readers of *Writing* get published. She wanted to help them sustain an illusion.

I had read Mr. Harbank's article on the subway coming to Gramercy Park that morning. I had read the other article—"Making Your Characters Breathe," by Hester Marrison—over coffee in the Park Luncheonette. I had not had time to show them to Phoebe, or Ivy, or any of the others involved. I didn't want to. Someone like Amelia Samson would get three paragraphs into the Harbank piece and have a stroke. Phoebe would declare war on Gramercy Park.

Writing may or may not be an art, depending on the writer. Selling that writing is a business. Like any other business, it has rules and customs. Knowing the rules and customs can be a great help to someone just beginning.

Not knowing the rules and customs—or, worse yet, knowing the wrong ones—can destroy someone.

"My people won't like it," I said. "More than that. My people won't stand for it, and they won't be associated with it."

We might have had a fight. It would have been appropriate. Fighting was the customary means of communication at Writing Enterprises. Unfortunately, we were interrupted. The door of Alida Brookfield's office opened and Jack Brookfield came flying through.

He *literally* came flying. It was as if someone had picked him up and tossed him into the hallway.

TWELVE

It brought everyone out. Writing Enterprises staffers crowded in from the back corridors, eager to see who and what had blown Alida's fuse this time. From their looks of cynical amusement, I decided this wasn't an anomaly. Alida held these exhibitions regularly. Alida might even enjoy them.

Alida didn't look like she was enjoying herself, but I knew that might not mean anything. She was standing over Jack Brookfield's body, prodding his bulging stomach with her toe. She had been crying. There were traces of mascara tears at the corners of her eyes. Anger and frustration, I thought, not sorrow. Alida Brookfield looked as if she'd never been sorry about anything.

She pulled her foot back and gave Jack a vicious kick in the side. "Get up," she said. "Get off the goddamn floor."

Jack Brookfield was beached. "I'm going to sue you for assault," he said. "I'm going to have your sagging ass."

"I'm going to have *your* ass," Alida said. "I'm going to haul myself into the men's room, I'll get pictures of what you do in the men's room, I'll get photostats of everything, all the records—"

Jack found the leverage he needed. He got to his knees, then to his feet. His suit was streaked with dirt and lint. His face was scratched and puffy.

"You're crazy," he told her. "You don't know what's been going on around here and you never will."

"You don't know when you've got it good," Alida said. "You

don't know when to leave well enough alone. You've got to have everything, you've got to leech, you impotent little fag—"

I heard a sigh in my ear and turned. Stephen Brookfield was standing right behind me. He had his hands in his pockets and a superior little smile on his face. He looked like a television villain at the moment of triumph, unaware that the hero's friends are already scaling the walls to effect a rescue.

It occurred to me I was always thinking of the Brookfields in terms of television, B movies, and third-rate paperback originals.

Stephen Brookfield was thinking of me as an audience. He nodded at his aunt and his brother and said,

"Remarkable example of a lemming, isn't she?"

"Lemming?"

"Well, someone's already dead. You'd think she'd go easy on that stuff until she knew who killed him."

I disliked Stephen Brookfield enough to be a nuisance. "You think Jack killed Michael?" I asked him.

He shrugged. "I think Jack might have killed Michael. That should be enough."

"Why should Jack kill Michael?"

"Why not?" He put his hands in my hair. I stepped as far away as I could with the crowd pressing in on me. He gave me a look that said he *knew* my reluctance was only temporary. They always *know* your reluctance is only temporary. They know it the way romance writers *know* the bogeyman in the closet is the fiction editor of *The New Yorker*.

Alida and Jack had squared off, but they had run out of words. They stood on opposite sides of the hall, their backs pressed against facing walls. Felicity Aldershot stood in the door to her office, looking from one to the other.

"Go back to your offices," Alida said. She didn't bother to raise her voice. "Get out of here."

The crowd around me started to disperse. The corridor was silent. When they got to their cubicles on the back corridors, they would probably lock themselves in and indulge in furious torrents of gossip, but for the moment they were being discreet.

Alida didn't look at them, or at Stephen, or at Felicity, or at Jack. She seemed to be staring at the ceiling. Jack was staring at her.

"Why I put up with this, I don't know," Alida said.

Felicity wasn't going to risk another outbreak. She moved forward and put her hand on Alida's arm, said something in Alida's ear. Alida straightened and began patting distractedly at her face and hair.

"I know, Fel," she said. "Oh, I know. I know."

"Touching, isn't it?" Stephen Brookfield said. He said it loud enough to be heard. Alida Brookfield ignored him. Jack, who did not think it was touching, pried himself away from the wall, faced Stephen, and let out all the murderous rage he had unsuccessfully tried to impose on Alida.

"You," he told Stephen, "are going to wind up with your throat cut."

"Jack thinks Alida killed Michael," Stephen said. "He thinks she's gone crazy. He thinks she's going to kill us off one by one."

Jack pushed past us. He elbowed Stephen out of the way. He was just tall enough so that his elbow caught Stephen in the diaphragm, winding him.

I didn't like Stephen any more than Jack did. I had also had enough for one morning. It was much too early—not even ten o'clock, if I could believe Felicity Aldershot's desk digital—and I wanted to be somewhere locked and quiet where I could think. Most mornings I'm not up at ten. I'm often not up at ten-thirty. One of the nice things about working freelance is the option to work from nine at night to five in the morning if it suits you.

I turned away from the sight of Alida Brookfield with her head on Felicity Aldershot's shoulder and made for the back corridor and my "office." I was halfway there when Janet caught up with me.

"I've been looking for you everywhere," she said. "You've got a phone call. A Mr. Carras." Janet looked harassed. "He says it's very, very urgent."

THIRTEEN

The first thing Nick said was, "Is this a secure line?"

I considered sitting on the rickety desk, decided it would collapse under me, and took the chair instead. I got a cigarette and lit it. I do not usually enjoy getting phone calls from Nick Carras. We met under strained circumstances. We developed what friendship there is between us under strained circumstances. Every time we meet, we conspire to strain the circumstances even more. Phoebe thinks we are made for each other—Phoebe went to high school with Nick in Union City, New Jersey, and nursed his ego by phone when he was at the Harvard Law School—but I haven't seen any sign of it. Besides, the man I was seeing before I started seeing Nick was a lawyer. I had had enough of lawyers. Once I started seeing Nick, I couldn't talk myself into seeing anyone else, but I wasn't sure that mattered. I might just be going through an isolationist period.

If Nick would stop insisting he was saving his (unlikely) virginity for the marriage bed, I wouldn't *have* to be going through an isolationist period.

I took three quick drags on my cigarette and made up my mind to keep this conversation *rational*. I reminded myself that Nick keeps his clean socks in the refrigerator. I said, "I am sitting under the light of a naked bulb in what was, until a few days ago, a utility closet. I have just been watching Installment Sixteen in 'The Continuing Holocaust.' I don't think this is a secure phone."

Nick said, "Oh." Then he paused. Then he asked, "Do you

think it's all right anyway? I mean, do you think anyone's listening in?"

"Nick, for God's sake. They're all listening in. The phone is probably tapped six times—each of them has tapped all the phones, and none of them knows the others have. Or they all know the others have but they think nobody knows they have— oh, never mind."

"What's going on over there?"

"You don't want to know. *I* don't want to know."

There was another pause. "The thing is," Nick said, "I think I do want to know."

"Why?" I thought this was another attempt to Show an Interest in My Life. Nick works very hard at that sometimes. He occasionally manages it even when he isn't thinking about it.

He wasn't thinking about it now. "I've got a couple of ladies in my office," he said.

"Women," I said automatically.

He corrected himself just as automatically. "Women," he said. "One black woman and one Jewish woman. The Jewish woman wants to know why you didn't eat the stuff she left out for you this morning."

"I was late. I stopped at the luncheonette when I got down here." No need to say anything about just having coffee.

Nick knew I had just had coffee. "We'll let it go at that," he said, letting me know Phoebe was listening. "The thing is, I could use a little information from where you are. I talked to Mr. Martinez, and I wasn't happy about the way he sounded. I don't think you're going to be very happy about it either."

"He's screaming treason," I said.

"Not that bad," Nick said. "To tell you the truth, I can't figure out why he isn't screaming murder. In fact, the whole thing's a little odd. He didn't even sound interested."

"You handed him a brand new suspect with a brand new motive and he didn't sound interested?"

"I didn't tell him about the motive," Nick said. "What do you take me for? But I don't think I handed him a brand new suspect. It's not just that he didn't sound interested. He didn't sound surprised."

I considered this. Martinez had not mentioned a mysterious black woman to me when he bought me pie and Perrier. Why wouldn't he mention it if he knew about it?

"There's something even odder than that," I said. "Janet must have seen her come in. Friday. Only I don't think Janet's said anything to anyone."

"You mean to the people who work there?"

"I mean to the Brookfields. Or Felicity Aldershot."

"Is that in character?"

I thought about Janet's pimples and Janet's greasy hair and Janet's avid, close-set eyes. "It's definitely out of character," I said. "Everybody in this place gossips about everybody else. Continually. Whether they have something to gossip about or not. If I had to guess, I'd say Janet was usually worse than most."

"Why?"

"Plain girls who mind being plain tend to compensate. Janet has to be one of those people who pay for their invitations with information."

"Men take her out to listen to her gossip?" Nick didn't believe it.

"Women have her around to listen to her gossip," I said.

Nick said, "Oh." He had never considered the possibility that plain women might have as much trouble making friends with women as they did with men. I didn't think he'd ever considered the possibility of plain women.

I was being unfair, and I recognized it. I have a tendency to make Nick the focus of neuroses developed in his absence in reaction to people he's never met. I stubbed out my cigarette—it had burned to the filter—lit another one, and prepared to get off the phone. When I start imagining other people's faces on Nick's body, it is time to get off the phone.

I started to say something about the work piled on my desk— there were a lot of manilla envelopes, presumably put there by Alida or Felicity Aldershot—when I heard a murmur of voices in the background and realized Nick was consulting. I pulled the envelopes into my lap. "Love and Money," the first one said. "Love Scenes that Sizzle, Scorch, and Score!" There was also "Researching the Historical—A Checklist." I opened that one. The first paragraph read, "If you've ever looked at one of those five-hundred-page sexy historicals and thought, 'I'd never be able to do all that research,' think again. There's a lot less research involved than you think!"

Verna Train was going to take one look at that and burn down the building.

I was either going to kill myself or develop a terminal ulcer.

Nick came back on the line. "There's something else," he said. "Her sister got a call this morning."

"Sister?" I assumed "her" meant Ivy.

"Her sister lives with her," Nick said. "Takes care of the kids. She left the kids with the sister and came into New York for the weekend."

"Oh," I said.

"Her sister called up this morning and said she'd had a call. From Alida Brookfield."

"Is this what you called up about?" I asked him. "Why didn't you tell me this in the beginning?"

"It wasn't all I called up about," Nick said. "I told you the other things I called up about."

"Right," I said. "What did Alida Brookfield call her about?"

"That's what we don't know. She wanted to make an appointment, but we don't know what the appointment is about."

"An appointment for when?"

"Quarter to five tomorrow." There was a little silence on the line, more consultation in the background. "You can tell her we'll be there, if you want."

"But Nick," I said.

"I've got to go," he said. "Phoebe brought lunch and your cat stowed away in the hamper and this is an office and there's such a mess—"

I looked at the dead receiver a few moments before putting it in the cradle. I could picture Camille popping out of the hamper with one of Phoebe's chicken wings in her mouth, causing havoc in Nick's office. I should have been amused. I was much too worried.

I was not worried about Alida Brookfield wanting to see Ivy. I could think of sensible explanations for that.

I couldn't think of a sensible explanation for Janet *not* telling everyone in the office about Ivy Samuels Tree, Mysterious Black Lady.

Mysterious Black *Woman*.

FOURTEEN

It would have been worse if I'd had any time. It *might* have been worse if I'd had any privacy. Since I had neither, I spent the afternoon in alternating states of confusion and frustration, occupied by problems that, as far as I knew, had nothing to do with the death of Michael Brookfield.

Writing magazine was meeting a printer's deadline. Even under the best circumstances, magazine staffs lead manic-depressive lives. Half the time they sit staring at the walls, doodling and daydreaming about the blockbuster bestseller they're going to write about The Business. They spend the rest of their time meeting printer's deadlines. The entire staff of *Sophistication* once stayed up for seventy-two hours—straight through, no naps or breaks for lunch—to meet a printer's deadline. Printers have a union with very strict regulations about overtime. The people who own printing businesses have developed a near mania on the subject of not having to pay overtime. Mechanicals must arrive at the plant with plenty of time to spare. If they don't, the magazine is charged a late penalty. The people who own magazines have developed a near mania on the subject of not having to pay late penalties. Add to this the inevitable: the freelance writers all got their articles in late; six people are out with flu in Columns and Departments alone; and the assistant in Production (the brand new Smith graduate with bulimia) can't proofread. All magazines are assembled in the four days immediately preceding a printer's deadline. On the day of the deadline, a messenger service is called. Having been so instructed, a man arrives at four-fifteen exactly to collect the package. He is then kept waiting an hour and twenty minutes while the Art Department dismantles and repastes pages twenty-four and twenty-five, which the Art Director thinks are Crooked.

The staff of *Writing* had a few extras to contend with. In the first place, there was me, my legs shoved under a desk designed for a dwarf, my mind presumably focused on a section not due till the *next* printer's deadline, leeching the energies of three second assistants in the Art Department so I could see What It Would Look Like. In the second place, there was Alida Brookfield. That scene in the hall was not an isolated incident in the life of Writing Enterprises—it wasn't even an isolated incident in the day. Alida kept appearing in the back corridors, an artist's conception away from breathing smoke and flame. She stopped in Columns and Departments and tore a piece on Targeting the Query Letter to shreds. She fired the Marketing Editor. She rewrote the Letter from the Editor three times, and insisted on having each version typeset, proofread, and pasted down before rejecting it. At three-thirty, she had another screaming match, complete with breaking glass. This time, it was Stephen she was after.

I would have kept my door shut if I could. I couldn't. There was no window. The fan did nothing but reposition stale air. The room was so small it made me feel like Alice after she'd eaten the little cake. I shut the door several times—once when I wanted to climb into the wardrobe and look around—but it never stayed shut more than a few minutes. I'd get halfway through a cigarette and begin to feel as if I were being strangled. I'd get up and open the door.

All I found in the wardrobe was a small hole, positioned shoulder height for someone five ten. I had to stoop to look through it. Phoebe, who is four eleven, would have had to stand on a box to look through it. Anyone looking through it would see a dirty swatch of pasteboard wall.

I tried to concentrate on the special section articles. I hadn't thought anything could be worse than that plot-by-blueprint nonsense. I was wrong. Consider the following advice from "Doing It with Dialogue":

> Romance is a genre that celebrates the emotions. Never forget that you're dealing with the wild, the passionate, the extraordinary—and that your dialogue should reflect this heightened state of awareness. A hero who calls the heroine "dear" is as tame as hubby at home—which means, no romance hero at all! Pull out all the stops! Indulge your most extravagant fantasies! Have you always wanted a tall, dark, handsome stranger to call you "a little spitfire"? It may never happen to you—but it can happen to your heroine!

A few paragraphs later, the author of this piece—one Ilona Darby—advises her readers to "use the exclamation point! Use it! Use it!"

The one piece of decent thinking occurred halfway through "Love and Money: Love Scenes that Sizzle, Scorch, and Score!" The writer suggested sitting down at the typewriter when the mood is on you and writing sex scenes to store for future use. This sounds appalling, but it actually makes sense. Writing a good category romance sex scene takes a certain kind of psychological preparedness. If you happen to wake up one morning in that admittedly bizarre state, I say use it.

If you ever find yourself in the offices of Writing Enterprises, I say find an excuse to go home. I didn't really need an excuse— Alida Brookfield wasn't paying me and couldn't very well keep me at my desk—but I did need a sop to my conscience. I didn't trust the woman. I didn't trust Felicity Aldershot, either. I was sure that as soon as I disappeared into the elevator, they'd be plotting how to sneak this stuff past me, into the section, and next to Phoebe's interview. Since I was to pass the mechanicals, they couldn't get everything by me forever, but I didn't want things to go that far. I didn't want to give them a legitimate excuse called "too close to deadline to change anything."

At five to six, things finally started to calm down. Felicity Aldershot stopped in to say good night. She had what should have been a fashionable cashmere coat buttoned and belted until it made her look like breakfast porridge. She was wearing three-hundred-dollar shoes in a style better suited to an arthritic grandmother. She couldn't have been thirty-five. She was doing her best to look eighty.

She smiled for the sake of politeness and said, "Alida thinks we ought to have a meeting. All of us and all of you."

"All of who?"

"All the romance writers," Felicity said. "And all the staff here."

I thought of Ivy, who couldn't be seen in public, and of Hazel Ganz, who lived in Parma, Ohio, and who would probably be snowed in at the Cleveland airport trying to get to New York. Then I thought of Amelia Samson and nearly burst out laughing. Alida Brookfield thought she knew how to throw a temper tantrum. Next to Amelia Samson, Alida Brookfield was a feeble-voiced domestic cat.

I told Felicity we could only get four out of six at a meeting. Felicity said she would discuss it with Alida. Then Felicity disappeared.

As soon as she was out of the office, I was on my feet. I got my pea coat from the single hanger in the wardrobe, shrugged into it, and started binding myself with scarves. There had been cautious predictions of more snow coming over the radio all day, and in New York the February wind is always particularly bad. I had a scarf that went around my neck and down my chest under my coat. I had another scarf that went around my neck over my coat.

I had *another* scarf that went over my shoulders and could be raised to cover my ears in periods of dire necessity. All these scarves were different colors. The nice, sober navy blue went inside the coat.

I was pulling on gloves when I heard the knock on the door. When I looked up at Marty Lahler, I thought he'd come in to deliver another message from Alida. A minute later I thought he'd come to confess to the murder. He was sweating so much his palms made water stains every time he rubbed them against his pants. His bald spot was oozing sweat into his ring of thin sandy hair. Every other inch of visible skin was dry. He was a paradigm of nervousness.

He waited until both my gloves were on before he approached my desk. Then he shoved his hands in his pockets, craned his neck until he could look me in the eye, and said, "You never had any lunch! I could take you to dinner!"

FIFTEEN

I should have said no. I am thirty-one years old. I know that look when I see it. I know what a disaster it can be to encourage that look when there is no hope. I even know what a disaster it can be to encourage that look when there *is* hope. I could not turn Marty Lahler down. He must have spent hours getting up the courage to walk into my office and ask me that question. Every minute of those hours showed in his face. I had the distinct feeling I was the first woman he'd asked out in years.

"I could take you to the Russian Tea Room," he said. He frowned. "If it isn't too far uptown," he amended.

He seemed to be on the verge of being defeated by the simplicities of Manhattan geography. I was panicking for another reason entirely.

"I'm not dressed for it," I told him. I meant it was too expensive. Alida Brookfield did not pay for Marty Lahler's suits. They came off the rack at Alexander's.

Marty Lahler had always wanted to take a woman to dinner at the Russian Tea Room. He fell back on the great Manhattan article of faith.

"Nobody cares what you wear in this city anymore," he said.

I almost sighed out loud. Marty Lahler wasn't familiar with the Russian Tea Room except as a fantasy. I knew it inside out. Phoebe is addicted to touristy restaurants. The Russian Tea Room is her second favorite after Mamma Leone's.

Dinner for two at the Russian Tea Room can cost sixty dollars. With wine, it can cost a hundred. We'd be seated faster, served better, and presented with more palatable food at Cabana Carioca or Wylie's. I could have told Marty that, but I would have been wasting my time. None of it mattered to him.

I looked into his thin, pointed, anxious face and promised myself I would buy a ticket on the first plane to Brazil the next time Phoebe suggested a project. Then I grabbed my tote bag and followed him out the door.

We had nothing to talk about. In the elevator, in the cab, in the line at the restaurant, we were practically silent. I tried everything I could think of. Marty Lahler didn't go to concerts, didn't go to movies, didn't even watch television. He hadn't read a book since leaving Queens College. He thought painting was "suspicious." He had never heard of the New York City Ballet. By the time we were seated—at an obscure table in a back corner on the second floor—I was beginning to wonder if he actually lived and breathed.

I fell back on my mother's favorite Prescription for Popularity. (My mother talks like this. She has had a great deal of experience chairing committees and browbeating the Weston, Connecticut, Town Council.)

I asked Marty Lahler about the work he did for Writing Enterprises.

The question came as such a shock to him, it drew his attention away from the red tinsel boas on the lamps.

"What I do at Writing Enterprises?" he said. "I do the books."

I considered breaking my water glass on the side of the table and eating the pieces.

"I know you do the books," I said. I forced a note of admiration into my voice. "It must be very interesting. Working with money, you know, and watching a business grow from a small concern to a large one. That sort of thing."

Marty Lahler frowned. "Sometimes it's hard," he said. "Like now, with all this foreign publishing stuff—"

"Yes, yes," I said. I said it because he paused. I didn't want any more pauses in the conversation.

"Do you know about paperback books?" he asked me. "You print a lot of them, and then you're supposed to sell two thirds of what you print, and if you sell more you didn't print enough. At least, that's what she told me."

"Alida Brookfield?"

Marty shook his head. "Miss Aldershot," he said. He gave me a funny look that was oddly comforting. It was the first sign of intelligence he'd displayed. "Miss Brookfield doesn't concern herself with things like that," he said. "She—she sets policy."

"You mean she doesn't know what the hell is going on?"

Marty laughed. I welcomed the break in the tension. "I think she's going through that thing women go through when they're older," he said. "I used to think that happened all at once, but my sister says it doesn't. She says it takes years." I didn't bother to tell him that, in a woman of Alida's age, those years would be safely over. It made him feel better to think there was a medical —rather than psychological—explanation for Alida's craziness.

"Anyway," he said. "Miss Brookfield doesn't do the day-to-day stuff anymore. She sets policy and the rest of us carry it out. Right now the policy I'm supposed to be carrying out is collating all the returns from overseas and making sure we sold what we were supposed to and no more and no less." He blinked. "Except I can't," he said.

"You can't?"

"The police came in and took it all away. The papers and things. They let me make photocopies of what I wanted so I could work on them, but I didn't get everything, so I'm stuck. And we've got a problem because we have to tell the plant how many to print in what languages—we have to tell them about everything, the magazines, the Newsletters, the new books—it's all so complicated—and we're always underestimating some countries and not having enough." He did his best to look judicious. "Of course, all we had of the books was six months' returns. But they should have been *indicative.*"

I wondered who'd taught him the word "indicative." I wasn't cruel enough to ask. I decided Alida was cheating the IRS. It was the only explanation I could think of for her having hired an accountant too fundamentally unintelligent and essentially inexperienced not to know what papers he needed to make a report.

"Did you underestimate everything?" I asked him. "Or did you overestimate some places?"

"We didn't overestimate anything," he said. He was very proud of it. "There were always more people who wanted our product than we'd expected."

"Well," I said. "That's nice."

We stared at each other. The conversation lay flapping and dying on the table between us.

Marty Lahler couldn't stand it any more than I could. He looked at the ceiling. He looked at the floor. He gripped his wine glass so hard I thought it would break. Then he exploded.

"She doesn't *pay* them anything," he said. "That's what the problem is. She doesn't pay any of us anything but they're her nephews, they're supposed to be executives, and she has them living in walk-ups and eating out of delis—" He stopped for breath. When he started again, he was considerably calmer. "Miss Aldershot has an employment contract," he said. "She's got everything written in. Bonuses and salary and everything." He leaned across the table, telling me a secret. "She makes forty thousand dollars a year." He was almost reverent—almost, because there was a thin gleam of envy in his eyes and an uncomfortably malicious undertone in his voice. "Last year, with the bonuses, she made over three times that."

"She made two hundred percent of her salary for bonuses last year?" That didn't make any sense. There wasn't a company in the world that did business like that.

Marty Lahler wasn't interested in bonuses. "The rest of them make their fifteen thousand and the clothes and five hundred a month for an apartment. She won't give them any more. That's why he was stealing—Mr. Michael Brookfield, I mean. He was fixing the books in Newsletters and only letting us have some of it. You can't rent a decent apartment in Manhattan on five hundred a month."

I had no trouble remembering what I had rented in Manhattan at five hundred a month. Marty had a point there.

"They could live in Brooklyn," I suggested. "Or Queens."

"*I* live in *Queens*," Marty said. "Nobody would live in Queens if they didn't have to." He sat back in his chair and stared over my head, as if he were watching a movie projected on the wall behind me for his private amusement. "You know," he said, "most places, accountants make a lot of money. They make a lot more money than fifteen thousand a year."

That might have started us on a real conversation. It might, at least, have been the beginning of Marty Lahler talking about himself. Very few people are boring when they let you know what they really feel, what they really want—instead of what they want you to think they feel and want. Unfortunately, at that moment the waitress came up to take our order. Marty retreated into the absorbing occupation of ordering everything on the menu.

He hardly said another word to me until he leaned from the
cab window to call good night, just before I disappeared into the
Byzantine labyrinth the Braedenvoorst calls a courtyard.

SIXTEEN

I reappeared eight hours later, breathing fire. I do not like to be
woken in the morning. I especially do not like to be woken by the
phone ringing in the kitchen—ringing untiringly, for minutes, as
if the caller knew I was asleep and was determined to wake me
up. In these circumstances, I usually arrive at the phone to find
my agent at the other end, which means I have to stifle my urge
to blow a police whistle into the receiver. My agent wouldn't
wake me for the world. She lets the phone ring forty times because, while she's calling me, she's also checking the particulars
of a contract for that sitcom writer she handles on the Coast.

This time, I found Martinez. Martinez likes working eight to
four, although he only manages that shift one week out of three.
He likes getting up at six. He eats breakfast.

"Meet you downstairs in twenty minutes," he said. "Got some
stuff to tell you."

"I've got to feed the cat," I said. "Come up."

"Can't come up. I'm alone."

I was about to ask him whether it was Anita or the police
department who didn't approve of his being alone with me in my
apartment, but the dial tone had already begun buzzing in my
ear. I replaced the receiver in the cradle and started shuffling
back to the bedroom wing. Camille dug her claws into the hem
of my flannel nightgown and let herself be dragged along. Cats

are very practical animals. Camille had been left without dinner last night until after ten. She had no intention of letting me get away before she had a full dinner dish to stand guard over.

When I got down to Martinez, I was wearing ragged jeans, a ten-year-old nylon turtleneck (I'd never found another turtleneck that hugged me quite that way), an extra-extra-large gray wool sweater that hung to just above my knees, and mismatched socks. Martinez noticed the socks.

"We'll get a cab," he said. "I'll take you to work. I'll tell you all about it. Fascinating group you've got there."

"For God's sake," I said.

"Anybody's sake you want, sweetheart."

"It's quarter to eight," I said. "I can't go down there at quarter to eight. Nobody will be there." Except Marty Lahler, I thought. If I went down to Writing Enterprises at some ridiculously early hour, Marty Lahler would be waiting for me just beyond the elevator doors. He'd be there even if he'd never been that early for work in his life.

"Besides," I said, "I don't want to go down there. If I could skip it today, I would."

"You had any coffee yet?"

"No."

"Cigarettes?"

I was holding a lit cigarette in my hand. "Number two," I said, waving it.

Martinez put his hands in the pockets of his down jacket. "I'll buy you breakfast at the Lincoln Square Coffee Shoppe," he said. "When you get to your third cup of coffee, I'll start talking sense."

I do not like people doing these things to me. The Lincoln Square Coffee Shoppe is directly across what looks like a six-lane highway from Lincoln Center. The six-lane highway is really the merging of Columbus and Amsterdam Avenues. The Lincoln Square Coffee Shoppe has very strong coffee and large plate glass windows looking out on the city. I *love* the Lincoln Square Coffee Shoppe.

I started tramping west along Seventy-second Street, determined to give in with bad grace. A thin wash of snow was coming down in the not-quite-dawn. The brownstones had frosted windows and small piles of snow on the windowsills. There was no traffic. I comforted myself with the thought that I didn't really like New York without traffic.

Martinez caught up to me when I turned south on Columbus. Seventy-second Street and Columbus combines East Side architecture with West Side outrage. Through the smoke gray windows of Betsey Johnson, I could see a group of mannequins dressed in red and black polka-dot versions of what Victorian prostitutes probably wore for underclothes.

Martinez caught up to me at Sixty-eighth Street and started pushing me down the block.

"Stephen Brookfield," he said. "I've been over and over it, and Stephen Brookfield is the key."

We got to the door of the Lincoln Square Coffee Shoppe. I marched inside. Since it was nearly deserted, I marched to the booth farthest from the door but still against the windows. The waitress must have seen my face as I walked in. She arrived with coffee before I had a chance to sit down.

"Stephen Brookfield," Martinez repeated, sliding into the bench on the opposite side of the booth.

I drank half the coffee. I motioned for the waitress. I drank the other half of the coffee while she stood over me. Then she gave me a refill.

I lit another cigarette and said, "*Michael* Brookfield. The key to this whole thing is *Michael* Brookfield."

Martinez shrugged. "What do you want to know about Michael Brookfield? He was an asshole. He was an embezzler. He's dead."

"Right," I said.

"He was even an asshole embezzler," Martinez said. "You know what he did? He ran that division, that newsletter thing. People sent in subscriptions for newsletters. Some of them sent the money in cash. He took the cash. It would have taken a genius to cover tracks like that. He was no genius."

"He didn't cover his tracks," I said. "Everybody knew about it. I mean *everybody*. And what about his girlfriend?"

"She's been in St. Moritz since December. She's found another Michael Brookfield. This one has family money."

"Bully for her," I said.

Martinez let out an exaggerated sigh. "Do you want to hear what I've got to tell you? Are you going to listen to me?"

The coffee had woken me just enough to give me access to my long-term memory. I dragged a few things out of there: pictures at a police exhibition, tableaux of a lecture course on the art of murder.

" 'The key to a murder is always in the life of the murder victim,' " I recited. "You told me that."

"I know I told you that. It's true ninety-nine percent of the time. This is the other one percent."

"How do you know it's the other one percent? He must have done something to get himself murdered."

"Michael Brookfield was an embezzler and an expensive-woman addict. No one is going to murder him for embezzling. The expensive woman is in St. Moritz."

"Then it's something else," I said.

"Of course it is," Martinez said. "Something he saw, or heard, or read. Something to do with that—that situation down there."

"Did you make Janet what's-her-name keep her mouth shut about Ivy?"

That made Martinez sit up straight. It made him do more than that. He lit a Camel. He put it out, took out a second, and lit that. He drummed his fingers on the table. I sat and watched him, wondering what it all meant. I had never seen him nervous before. Even when he was handing me police department information I had no right to have, he wasn't nervous.

He looked out the window at Columbus Avenue. "I thought she was a friend of yours," he said.

"I met her for the first time Friday. And that's not the point."

"What is the point?"

I was on my third cup of coffee. I was awake. My mind was working double time. My paranoia was to the front and pumping. The things Martinez was doing only made sense one way. The way they made sense made me think I'd never really liked him at all. It reminded me I hadn't liked him in the beginning.

Make it simple, I thought. Martinez himself had told me that. Make it simple. Martinez was making it more complicated. Every time he talked to me about the murder, it got more complicated.

"I think you're setting me up," I said.

He got very stiff. "What do you mean, setting you up?"

"Ivy was there at the right time. There are suggestions of blackmail. Nobody would murder Michael Brookfield because he was an embezzler. The girlfriend is in St. Moritz. But someone might have murdered Michael Brookfield if he were a blackmailer."

Martinez got even stiffer. "There isn't any evidence of blackmail," he said. "Don't think we haven't looked for it, either. There isn't a dime in his bank account that can't be explained by his salary or his embezzling. Not a dime."

"You knew Ivy had been there. Janet knew Ivy had been there. Everybody at Writing Enterprises is a gossip, as far as I can tell. Janet hasn't said anything to anybody."

"I didn't ask anybody named Janet not to say anything to anybody."

"Right," I said.

He put his cigarette out. His eyes were very dark and very cold. "Do you intend to tell me what I'm supposed to be doing? Or am I supposed to guess?"

"You keep telling me things," I said. "Things about the Brookfields, about the 'situation' at Writing Enterprises. You want to focus my attention on that. You don't care about that. If I concentrate on the Brookfields, you can concentrate on Ivy. You can build a case and make an arrest and not worry about any interference from me."

"Shit," Martinez said.

"That's exactly what I think it is," I said. "Shit."

"Just tell me this," Martinez said. "Stephen Brookfield is clean. He makes fifteen grand a year, he lives in a rattrap, and he's clean. Does that make sense to you? Jack is stealing the petty cash, Michael is cooking his books, but Stephen is clean. Does that make sense to you? Tell me. Just tell me."

SEVENTEEN

I didn't want to tell him anything. I left him with the coffee and the bill and ran out to hail the first cab cruising south. I got one very quickly. If I hadn't, I might have started to walk. I didn't want to stand out on the street, waiting for Martinez to catch up with me.

I was more than halfway to Gramercy Park before I realized I'd started a fight for no reason at all. I'd started a fight because I wanted to start a fight. Not that I wasn't suspicious—God only knows Martinez wasn't making much more sense than anyone else—but I wasn't being fair, either. I didn't want to be fair. I wanted—

—an out. It hit me just as I was paying off the cab driver on Park Avenue South. From the beginning all I'd wanted was an out. I didn't want to play detective. I didn't want to write a book about the second murder case I'd been involved in. I didn't want to see any more pictures of myself in the New York *Post*. I didn't like murders and I didn't like murderers and I didn't like this feeling that everything was coming down on my head. Last time, I explained the roof-caving-in feeling as a result of being suspected of the crime. This time, no one suspected me of anything, unless you counted the main crime reporter for the *Post*, which I didn't. If the roof was caving in, it was because I wasn't suited for this work. I might be suited for researching and writing up crimes after they'd happened, but I had no business involving myself in ongoing investigations.

If I wanted out badly enough to start a full-scale war with the detective lieutenant in charge of a murder case I was even marginally connected with, I ought to *get* out.

I got into the one working elevator just before the doors closed. I leaned against the door and lit a cigarette under the No Smoking sign. The only way to get out was to quit my work with Writing Enterprises. I couldn't see any way to do that. Phoebe and the rest of them had a legitimate problem. They had a legitimate lien on my time and energy. I owed those people. Some of them had helped when I was first starting out in New York and making no money. Some of them had helped when I was suspected of murdering Myrra Agenworth. Some of them had helped afterward, when I was first trying to write the book for Doubleday and coming apart at the seams every time I approached the material.

The elevator stopped on twenty and I got out. The reception area was empty. Either I was early or Janet never spent any time at her desk. I decided both halves of that statement were true.

I started down the hall corridor, half-walking, half-running. Felicity Aldershot was in her office. She looked up as I came by, waved, and went back to the papers on her desk. I had a pile of articles on my desk, all with questions penciled in the margins. I would have to take the questions up with Alida and Felicity sometime. I would have to check the mechanicals. I would have to fight about the placement of ads. I could not just stop coming in to the office.

There was a light in Jack Brookfield's office. The door was open. Inside, a voice I recognized was going on and on, filling the air with pointed little jabs.

"I've got a lawyer," the woman was saying. "I've got a lawyer and I've got evidence and I'm going to sue."

It took me a while to place her. Then it hit me. The woman with the social worker's face. Mrs. Haskell. The woman who'd sent her manuscripts to Literary Services and thought she'd been cheated.

"I assure you," Jack Brookfield was saying, "everything has been done in accordance with our contract. No matter how eminently publishable your manuscript is, there is no way to guarantee publication. Publication depends on editors. Editors have their private tastes and opinions, just like anyone else. Publishing is not a monolithic—"

His voice trailed off. I rounded the corner and stepped into the back corridor. Marty Lahler was just coming out of his office. I did a one-hundred-eighty-degree turn and headed back in the direction I'd come.

There had been a light on under Alida's door when I first came in. Alida was probably at her desk. I'd learned a few things from my short association with Writing Enterprises. One of the things I'd learned was that Alida Brookfield was cheap.

I couldn't stay away from the office forever. I might, however, be able to stay away for a while. Long enough, for instance, to let Martinez get the murder cleared up. Mechanicals and advertisements had to be handled in the office. Manuscripts I could edit sitting in a bath.

"Publication," Jack Brookfield was saying, "is difficult to achieve at the best of times, because the publishing community, at least in its national incarnation, is so limited and close-knit. Now, if you try—"

Felicity Aldershot was on the phone. ". . . figures for the first half of last year," she was saying, "giving us an idea of the overruns and the distribution . . ."

Stephen Brookfield passed me in the hall. He looked more deathly pale than usual.

I got to Alida Brookfield's door. I knocked twice and got no answer. I knocked again. That time, the door pushed open, creaking on its hinges. It was so much like an American International horror movie, I almost giggled.

Instead, I stifled nerves and merriment and stepped inside. Alida was sitting in her swivel chair, her back to the door.

The ends of the typewriter ribbon were dangling over the chair back, blowing in the slight breeze from a partially opened window.

I didn't feel, or think, or react. There was nothing to feel or think or react *to*.

Even when I had backed out of the office and turned to face the hall, even when I had seen Ivy hesitating midway down the corridor to the reception area, I wasn't able to feel anything but numb.

EIGHTEEN

It was worse than the first time—faster, colder, more efficient. The police seemed less like an invading army than a continuous presence. The hallway was cordoned off. The staff was pulled out of its offices and herded into the reception area. The fingerprint men and the photographers and the man from the medical examiner's office went back and forth, making notes in pocket notebooks.

Martinez wasn't talking to me. He brushed by me twice without even looking at me. He finally handed me over to Tony Marsh. Tony Marsh's Boy Scout face looked shell-shocked.

"He doesn't seem to want to ask you any questions," Tony said. "I'm supposed to ask you questions. I don't know what questions to ask you."

"Maybe I should just make a statement," I said. I was having a hard time keeping my eyes up. My head wanted to fall to my chest. My body wanted to go slack. My exhaustion had to be emotional, but that didn't make it feel better. I was physically sick with it.

Tony was pleased with the idea of taking my statement. He knew how to take a statement. He spread his shorthand notebook on Michael Brookfield's desk, picked up his pencil, and waited patiently.

Michael Brookfield's office had been under police seal. I had never seen it. I looked around and decided I hadn't missed anything. It was a medium-sized office, neither shabby nor spectacular. It was absolutely clean. There was no evidence Michael Brookfield had ever done any work here.

"Did you clean it out like this?" I asked Tony. "It looks barren."

"It was barren," Tony said. "I mean, everything's here that was here in the beginning. In the beginning of the investigation, that is. We didn't take anything out."

"Maybe she was right," I said. "Maybe Michael didn't do any work."

"Who said Michael didn't do any work?"

"Alida." I waved my hand toward the hall. "The one who got it this time."

Tony Marsh frowned. He had been on the force one year and three months. His first major case involved a corpse found on the floor of my old one-room apartment. He had been attached to the twentieth precinct. Now he was attached to some other precinct—I had no idea which one took in Gramercy Park—and here I was again. Asking questions. Not giving a regular statement. He gestured at his notebook.

"Maybe you ought to start from the beginning," he said. Tony Marsh, being a Boy Scout, is always very polite.

"There isn't any beginning," I told him. "I knocked on her door. It opened by itself. I walked in. She was sitting in the chair."

"You didn't touch her." Statement, not question. He was learning in the police department.

"I did not touch her," I said.

"How did you know she was dead?"

"I saw the typewriter ribbon," I said. "The ends of it were dangling over the back of the chair."

"Over the back of the chair?" Tony Marsh said.

"I don't understand about the typewriter ribbon," I said. "How can you strangle anybody with a typewriter ribbon? Why doesn't it break?"

"Silk typewriter ribbon," Tony Marsh said. "The lieutenant thought the same thing but we tried it out. We didn't strangle anybody, you know, but we tried it out. Pulling it. It doesn't break."

"Somebody killed two people with them," I said, "so I suppose they don't break."

"You said you saw it hanging over the back of the chair," Tony Marsh said again.

"That's right," I said.

"And you didn't move the chair," he said.

"I didn't move the chair. I didn't touch anything." I lit a cigarette and watched him through the smoke. His face was tense and disturbed. His fingers were tapping arrhythmically against the desk.

"You know anything about this Alida Brookfield?" he asked me. "Anything about her habits?"

"I know she was crazy," I said. "She screamed at people— mostly her nephews. She had tantrums."

"You know anything about money?" Tony Marsh said. "You know anything like how much money she'd be carrying with her, you know, cash, on a normal day?"

"Cash?"

"Walking around money. Like in her wallet."

I put my cigarette in the ashtray. "Officer Marsh," I said. "What's going on around here?"

Officer Marsh was very solemn. "There's been a homicide committed," he said. "We're investigating the commission of a homicide."

NINETEEN

It was Nick who finally told me what was going on. He was in the reception area when I finished with Tony Marsh. He had one arm around Ivy Samuels Tree. He had a legal-sized manilla folder in his other hand. As soon as he saw me, he stood up, disengaged himself from Ivy, and hustled me into a far corner of the room.

"They're going to arrest her," he said. "They're going to *arrest* her." He made it sound as if the earth had just been declared flat by act of Congress.

"Is that what you're doing here?" I asked him. "She called you?"

"She called me. I would have come if you called me."

"I didn't call you," I said. "All the time I was coming down here this morning, I was thinking I wanted to stay home. I should have stayed home."

"*Ivy* should have stayed home," Nick said. "I told her I didn't want her down here. Shit, I told her I didn't want her within five miles of Park Avenue South. And here she is."

"Why?"

"She says she wanted to straighten it out once and for all."

"Good lord."

"I know," Nick said. "I *know.*"

I sat down on a bench with a cracked plastic cushion and lit another cigarette. My lungs were beginning to feel the way they do after a long night of drinking and poker. I was getting a nicotine headache. Nick hovered over me, distracted, bringing no comfort.

"Crazy stuff is going on around here," he said.

"Do you know how they found the body?" I asked him. "And
. . ." I thought hard. I was so tired things kept slipping in and
out. "Something about money," I said finally. "Cash. How much
cash she had on her."

Nick gave me a sideways look. "Cash," he said. "There wasn't
any cash. That was the point."

"There wasn't any cash?"

"Weren't any credit cards, either," Nick said, "but that's apparently all right. According to the English lady, Miss Brookfield
didn't *have* any credit cards."

"No cash and no credit cards," I repeated.

"Her pocketbook was open on the floor," Nick said. "Her
pockets had been turned out."

I sat bolt upright. *"Robbery?"* I said. "Nick, that's ludicrous.
That's ridiculous. Nobody tied a goddamned typewriter ribbon
around her neck for the cash in her purse—"

"Nobody's saying anybody did."

"Somebody's saying something," I said. "Pocketbook open on
the floor, pockets turned out, no cash. What about the position
of the body? Back to the door?"

"Facing the door." He saw the odd look I gave him and
shrugged. "Conversation overheard in a hallway," he said.

"When I went in there the back of the chair was facing the
door."

"What did you do after you went in there?"

I gave it a moment's thought. "I backed out and shut the door.
I made sure it caught. I went into Felicity Aldershot's office and
tried to call the police. I don't know where Felicity was. I
couldn't figure out how to get an outside line. I came out here
and used the one on that desk." I pointed across the room.

"What did you do until the police arrived?" Nick said.

"Sat out here and waited."

"Plenty of time."

"Are you trying to tell me someone went into that office and
robbed Alida Brookfield's dead body?"

"I'm not trying to tell you anything," Nick said. "Somebody could have robbed the body after they murdered her, or robbed her and then turned her into a dead body, or come in and moved the chair after you'd left, or maybe she didn't have any cash on her at all, or—"

"Mr. Carras?"

Nick straightened up immediately. Martinez was standing directly behind him, waiting patiently. Martinez's voice was ceremonially polite. He didn't look at me.

"I believe we have some formalities to take care of," Martinez said.

"Have you taken Miss McKenna's statement?" Nick said. "Her statement may have some bearing—"

"We've taken Miss McKenna's statement," Martinez said.

Nick wasn't going to fight any more than he had to, not at this stage. Martinez turned to cross the room and Nick turned with him. I could see Ivy on the other side of the reception area, huddled in a chair. What *had* she come for? And if she *had* to come, why hadn't she waited until her afternoon appointment? Why show up at some ungodly hour of the morning when no one expected her?

I got off the bench and headed for Janet's desk. I'd left my pea coat on the back of her chair. I wanted to get it and put it on. I wanted to catch a bus back to Central Park West. I'd made my statement. Martinez had made his decision. I knew he'd let me go.

On the far side of the room, Martinez was making the formal arrest. At the entrance to the corridor, Tony Marsh was escorting Mrs. Haskell out. Martinez had just come to the part about "arresting you for" when Mrs. Haskell planted herself in the center of the room, threw back her head, and started shouting.

"I don't care what's been going on around here," she said. "I'm going to impound your records and I'm going to force an audit and I'm going to get what's coming to me."

TWENTY

It was an odd moment. It was made odder still by the fact that
we all witnessed it. The arrival of the police had set up a Gulf
Stream effect. People drifted in and out of the reception area, in
and out of halls, in and out of offices. In the back corridor, they
were ostensibly trying to meet the printer's deadline, though I
doubt they were getting much work done. Periodically, one anon-
ymous anorectic editorial assistant or another would erupt into
the reception area, lay hands on one of the principals, and drag
him or her away in the direction of the Art Department. For
some reason, when Mrs. Haskell made her announcement, all the
principals were in one place. They were huddled together under
the huge poster of the cover of *Writing*'s fiftieth anniversary
issue, the one with the inkwell and the quill pen and the headline
that read 101 *new* WAYS TO BREAK INTO PRINT.

Mrs. Haskell stopped everything. Poor, fat Jack went bright
red. Sweat poured down his double chin into his collar. Damp
perspiration patches spread over his shirt. Felicity, halted mid-
sentence in a lecture on Organization, blinked twice and started
looking around the room, as if she wasn't sure where the interruption had come from. Stephen Brookfield looked sick. Martin
Lahler looked ready to cry. Even Martinez and Ivy and Nick,
who should have had more important things on their minds, fixed
their attention on Mrs. Haskell and showed no inclination to get
back to business.

Mrs. Haskell, realizing she'd *finally* got someone's attention,
responded as expected. She drew herself erect, folded her arms

across her chest, clasped her large shabby purse over her stomach, and said,

"Four hundred fifty dollars I put into this. Eighteen months I put into this. *You're not going to get away with it.*"

Equal and opposite reaction: the second speech reversed the effect of the first. Everyone but Marty Lahler started talking at once. Marty Lahler sat down on a bench under a sign that asked DO *you* HAVE WHAT IT TAKES TO BE A WRITER? and curled himself into a ball. The others ignored him.

"What's she talking about?" Felicity Aldershot asked. "Who does she *belong* to?"

"All that work," Stephen Brookfield giggled. "All that *work.*"

Poor, fat Jack went into his patented executive act. He rushed at Mrs. Haskell, patted her arm, and started murmuring double-speed inanities. Mrs. Haskell wanted no part of him. Neither did Felicity Aldershot.

"What's she going to sue us for?" Felicity Aldershot said.

Mrs. Haskell turned on the venom. "Literary Services," she said. "*I* know what you're doing. *I* know how to prove it. I'm going to get your records and I'm going to get your accounts and I'm going to shut you down."

Felicity reached into the pocket of her checked wool dress and came up with a pack of cigarettes. She took one out and lit it. She stared at Jack.

"Shut what down?" she demanded.

The back of Jack's jacket was sodden. His face was oddly purple. He seemed incapable of looking at anything but the floor.

"Literary Services," he mumbled. "Mrs. Haskell here is under the impression—"

"I'm not under any impression," Mrs. Haskell said. "I *know.*"

"Tell me about it," Felicity said. She was speaking to Jack. "Just what does Mrs. Haskell *know?*"

Jack took a deep breath. "Repeats," he said. "I'm afraid I've been unable to convince her we do not—ah—do not deliberately give misleading advice to our clients. So their books don't sell. So they have to come back to us."

"A new fee every time," Mrs. Haskell said. "A full fee every time."

"A full fee every time," Felicity repeated. "What does this have to do with anything?"

Felicity was still looking at Jack, but Mrs. Haskell had had enough of being the invisible woman. She marched across the room and planted herself in front of Felicity, leaving Jack stranded in the middle of the carpet like an expiring dolphin.

"Policy," Mrs. Haskell said. "What we have to prove is policy. How many people repeat their submissions? How many people are published? How long's it been going on?" Mrs. Haskell smiled. "Records," she said. "And accounts."

"Records," Felicity Aldershot said. Her voice was faint. Her face was very white.

"Prove how much they paid you," Mrs. Haskell said.

As far as Felicity was concerned, Mrs. Haskell had never stopped being the invisible woman. She walked around her the way she'd skirt a piece of furniture, strode up to Jack, and grabbed his lapels.

"Accounts," Felicity said. "Accounts. Of all the times to land us in a goddamn *lawsuit*, in a goddamn *attachment*, you incompetent little *idiot*—"

Stephen Brookfield burst out laughing. He laughed until he vomited into the clay pot that nurtured a dying avocado tree.

TWENTY-ONE

That should have been the end of it. Martinez had made his arrest. Writing Enterprises was in shambles. Nick was busy on the part of a murder case he understood: preparing for court. I went home that afternoon fully expecting to hear nothing more of that mess until I was called to testify for one side or the other. I did not think Ivy Samuels Tree had killed Michael and Alida Brookfield—the explanation was entirely too neat and the circumstances too fortuitous—but it was not my problem. My problem was convincing my editor at Doubleday that a book by me on the Brookfield murders would *not* be the greatest commercial offering since chunky peanut butter. In a sane world, *Writing* magazine would have suspended publication for a month for reorganization and the murderer would have left well enough alone. Writing Enterprises, however, had no known connection to a sane world.

I had a week of bliss. I marshaled my courage and told my doctor I weighed one hundred nine, hadn't fasted for two months, and couldn't stop the slide. My doctor marshaled his tact, didn't lecture me, and started a series of tests to determine why I couldn't fatten up. Coming back from his office, I stopped on Fifth Avenue and bought two pounds of Godiva chocolates (raspberry, strawberry, and lemon creams, plus soft butterscotch) and another pint of Devon cream for the cat. The cat was duly appreciative.

Phoebe made me dinner three times. I bought her lunch at Mamma Leone's once. She confessed herself relieved to be rid of the *Writing* magazine special romance section. She hinted I'd given up too easily on the Brookfield murders. I ignored her.

My agent called to say I'd been offered a chance at a Screenplay (to my agent, all assignments with fees in five figures are Capitalized) and did I want to take it. I said a rude word in her ear.

Muffy Arnold Whitney, my old editor at *Sophistication*, called to ask if they could do an interview with me. I, after all, had a major book coming out. (How *Sophistication* decided the Agenworth book was going to be major, I don't know.) Also, I was the first woman full-time true crime writer in history. I was a Role Model. Muffy Arnold Whitney had given me a lot of work over the years. I tried to be polite. It was difficult. I told her about Ann Rule and *The Stranger Beside Me* and hung up.

Nick called.

It was Nick's call that started the avalanche sliding again. He phoned nine-thirty Saturday night to ask if he could camp out on my floor and have breakfast with me Sunday. I didn't mind the timing—I do things like that to people and I am comfortable when they do them to me—but I didn't like the tone of his voice. I should have realized that, as Ivy's defense attorney, he would have Ivy's defense on his mind. He would have it on his mind particularly because it was going to be his first murder defense.

"I'd feel a lot better about it," he told me, "if it didn't look impossible on the face of it."

"You think it's going to be impossible to get her off?"

"I think it would be impossible to convict her," Nick said. "I guess they're going to go for a blackmail motive, but there isn't any blackmail motive. There isn't even as much blackmail motive as there was the last time."

He gave me a sour look. I had the good sense to blush into my glass of wine. I didn't like to think about the blackmail business in the Agenworth case. It had claims on making the list for the top ten most embarrassing farces in history.

"The fact is," Nick said, "there isn't any blackmail evidence.

Martinez admits there isn't any blackmail evidence. What's the DA going to bring into court?"

"Assumption?" I suggested. "There was no blackmail but Ivy thought there was blackmail?"

"Couldn't prove it. Jury wouldn't buy it. And here's another thing. Ivy's out on bail."

"I thought you couldn't get out on bail on a murder charge."

"Nothing's hard and fast," Nick said. "Basically, though, on first and second they lock you up and keep you locked up. They didn't charge her with second. They charged her with man-slaughter."

"Manslaughter? Right off the bat? Without plea bargaining?"

"Right off the bat," Nick said. "I know it's screwy, McKenna. I've been over it a dozen times. How're they going to justify manslaughter? Those people were strangled with typewriter rib-bons, for God's sake. Somebody had to have done it deliberately. Somebody had to get hold of the typewriter ribbons. There were typewriter ribbons in Alida Brookfield's office, but whoever killed Michael brought one with him. Typewriter ribbons are not the kind of thing Ivy carries around in her purse, so when she flies into a heat of passion—"

"Were they office typewriter ribbons?" I asked him. "The kind the staff always uses?"

"Yeah," Nick said. "That's all sealed up. You see what I mean?"

"I see Martinez must have had a tame ADA," I said. "Who bought this mess, anyway? It's Swiss cheese."

"It's worse than Swiss cheese. It's a hot air balloon." Nick turned over on his stomach. The cat climbed on his shirt and made herself comfortable in the hollow made by the small of his back. Being used to the cat, Nick left her there. "I keep thinking there has to be a catch," he said. "The whole thing's so impossi-ble, it can't be true. They have to have something else. If they didn't, they'd never have made an arrest."

"What could they have?"

"How am I supposed to know? I've got a guy in the police

department, but he hasn't come up with anything. I've got someone in the Manhattan DA's office, but all she'll say is they're
proceeding with the blackmail motive. I don't think she's lying to
me. I think, for public consumption, they *are* proceeding with
the blackmail motive."

"The New York Police Department is not the court of Con-
stantine and Helen," I said.

"Spanish," Nick said. "Not Greek, Spanish. It's that friend of
yours. I'm sure of it."

Martinez was no longer a friend of mine, but I didn't want to
mention it. I said the only sensible thing I could think of. "It's
the second visit. What was Ivy doing there? What was she doing
there in the morning?"

"You want to know what she says?" Nick asked. "She *says* she
got a call asking her to be there. She was staying at Phoebe's.
Phoebe says she got a call, too. According to Ivy, Alida Brookfield
wanted an urgent meeting on the article Michael was writing
before he died."

"Alida called Ivy?" I said. "But Nick, Alida didn't know who
ran what in her own business. She couldn't even keep her nephews apart. How would she know enough about some article Michael was writing for the romance newsletter to call up Ivy—"

"She didn't call herself," Nick said. "Some secretary called.
Probably that receptionist."

"But—" I said.

That was when the phone rang. I went into the kitchen to
answer it.

Felicity Aldershot had no intention of suspending publication
of *Writing* magazine for a month. Felicity Aldershot had no intention of postponing the special romance section.

Felicity Aldershot wanted to see me in her office first thing
Monday morning.

TWENTY-TWO

It felt like instant replay, even with some of the characters missing. This time it was Felicity Aldershot who sat behind the ornate mahogany monstrosity of a desk. Jack, Stephen, and Martin Lahler stood at the side. As soon as I came in, Felicity rose, gestured to the conversational grouping, and led the way there. Instead of leaving, as Martin and Felicity herself had the first day, Jack, Stephen, and Martin followed us to the bar. Martin poured me a cup of coffee.

"We had to talk to the lawyers," Felicity said, "but everything's straightened out now. I think we can get back to work."

Jack and Stephen sat side by side, grinning tension. Jack was sweating. Stephen looked more than ever like the down-at-heels traitor in a Graham Greene novel. Neither met my eye. Their aunt was dead. It would be logical to expect them to have inherited her authority. Instead, they were under the control of another woman.

Felicity Aldershot had blossomed. When I first met her, she was deferential and indirect. She had deflected attention from what control she had exercised—which had probably been considerable—by appearing overworked and faintly ingratiating. There was nothing deferential or ingratiating about her now. She was a natural commander.

She took the coffee Martin handed her and didn't bother to smile.

"Maybe I should explain things," she said. "I suppose you have cause to wonder if we have the means, or the ability, to go ahead as planned. Or the authority, for that matter."

I said something unintelligible. Means, ability, and authority were not what I was wondering about. *Balls* were what I was wondering about. Were they really going to go ahead as if nothing had happened? Did Felicity really expect me, and everyone else connected in any way to Writing Enterprises, to behave as if it were business as usual?

Not quite. Felicity had decided that at least I deserved an explanation.

"Miss Brookfield's will," she said, "was designed to make Writing Enterprises an independent and autonomous entity. Independent of the whims and wishes of the people who work here, that is."

This sounded so blatantly feudal, I decided she didn't mean it.

"Instead of leaving the business to an heir or heirs, the will established a trust. The trust will run Writing Enterprises. In fact, all the trust can do is run Writing Enterprises."

"I thought a trust was money," I said. "Or investments."

"Writing Enterprises is an investment. A trust has trustees. The trustees will run Writing Enterprises."

I said, "Ah," because I didn't know what else to say. Stephen got up and put a slug of Chivas Regal in his coffee.

"Why don't you just tell her?" he said. He turned to me. "She's got a contract. A ten-year employment contract. Under the terms of the will, the trustees can't alter the terms of the contract unless she agrees." He gave Felicity a sour look. "They can't fire her, either."

"Nobody's talking about firing anybody," Jack said nervously. *"Nobody's* talking about firing *anybody."*

Stephen tasted his coffee and found it weak. He added another slug of Chivas. "Old Alida was a female supremacist," he said. "The world would be a much better place if it were run by women."

Felicity smiled a thin, tolerant smile. "The world would be a much better place if it were run by Alida," she said. "That's all over and done with, Stephen."

"A lot of things are over and done with," Stephen said.

Felicity ignored him. "Writing Enterprises is not over and done with," she promised me. "We want to go ahead with the September issue. We want to go ahead with the romance section. We're just going to have to do it in two weeks instead of four."

"Two weeks," I said. I thought of the pile of manuscripts probably lying on the desk in my "office." I could not deal with them in two weeks. I didn't even want to. I wanted to spend the next two weeks at Writing Enterprises the way I wanted herpes. The Brookfields were crazy. Felicity Aldershot made me cold. None of these people cared about the two murders. Felicity didn't even seem to have noticed them.

"I've been thinking about your problems with the articles we commissioned," Felicity said. "In fact, I spent all last week thinking about them. I don't want a fight on that right now."

It looked like a way out, so I took it. "You're either going to have to fix those articles or you're not going to have the interviews," I said. "They won't be associated with that kind of thing."

"They won't have to be. We'll throw the articles out."

"Throw them out?"

"As you've undoubtedly guessed, I will be taking over the editing of *Writing* magazine. I've been doing quite a bit of it over the last few years—"

"Doing quite a bit of everything," Stephen muttered.

Felicity sailed over him. "There won't be any long-term problems," she said. "There are a couple of short-term ones, however. We missed the printer's deadline with the issue before the one you're working on. We won't get that to the plant until today, which means very high late penalties. I don't intend to be late a second time. The agreements we signed with the writers of the articles in question guaranteed twenty percent kill fees. I don't intend to let that money go down the drain. I want to normalize the situation, Miss McKenna."

I couldn't stand it any more. "You can't normalize this situation," I said. "Two people are *dead.*"

Felicity Aldershot looked no more than mildly surprised. "This is a corporation," she said. "Exxon doesn't close down if one of its employees dies. It doesn't close down if the chairman of the board dies."

"This isn't Exxon."

"The legal status of a corporation," Felicity Aldershot said, "is independent of its size."

She thought this answered everything. She was so sure it answered everything, she almost convinced me. I got out a cigarette and lit it. I wondered what she expected me to do now.

Jack must have thought I was angry. He leaped into the conversation, determined to calm me down.

"It's like show business," he said. "The show must go on." He produced this cliché as if it were enough to convince anybody of his wisdom, perspicacity, and common sense. He almost started Stephen on another laughing fit.

"About the articles," Felicity Aldershot said.

"That section better be the bonanza everybody expects it to be," Stephen Brookfield said. "If it isn't, we're all going to look like idiots."

"We'll throw the articles out," Felicity Aldershot said. "Your people can write their own articles. They can say anything they want to say as long as it isn't likely to get us sued."

"There's a catch," Stephen said. "There always is around here."

"There isn't a *catch.*" Felicity was finally angry. It didn't last long. "I don't intend to pay any more for those articles than I originally offered, that's all. I'll offer your people the same fee I offered the original writers, minus the twenty percent I owe on kill fees. That is hardly a *catch.*"

"Maybe it's just cheap," Stephen said.

"Will your people think it's cheap?" Felicity asked me.

I hesitated. This situation was so bizarre, I was so convinced Ivy had *not* killed Alida and Michael Brookfield and one of these people had, all I wanted was an excuse. Unfortunately, I knew what "my people" would think of Felicity's offer. My people would love it. My people wouldn't care if they were paid nothing. They were so sick of what they called "all the nonsense written about romance," so tired of listening to people talk about romance novels as something any illiterate with the price of a typewriter could write and publish, they would kill for the chance to set the record straight.

They'd kill *me* if I tried to deprive them of it.

TWENTY-THREE

Felicity Aldershot was no Alida Brookfield. She was not crazy. Her temper was under control. Her nerves were under control, too. She must have given the word to the others. I was to be treated with Kindness, Courtesy, and Cooperation.

Jack took me back to my office. He brought a fresh pot of coffee and a clean cup. He hopped when he walked, starting jelly waves in his torso that slithered like a Slinky going downstairs.

"We aired it out this morning," he said, when he opened the door for me. "It was beginning to smell a little musty." Then, as if this were not enough, he gave me a big toothy smile and said, "We'd move you into a larger office, but there isn't one. The police made a shambles of everything."

I knew that was only half the truth, but I wasn't going to press it. I was sure the police hadn't made a shambles of Felicity's old office, but I didn't want to occupy it, either. Besides, it was always so hard for me to be rough on poor, fat Jack. He wanted so badly to be beaten up. I wanted so badly not to give him the pleasure.

I sat on the inadequate desk chair and poured myself a cup of coffee. Over my head, what had been a naked bulb was now covered with a green and yellow Chinese paper lampshade. Jack noticed me notice it. He acted as if I'd made his day.

"We tried to fix it up," he said. "Felicity is very big on the importance of working conditions. Working conditions determine productivity."

"Do they really?" I said.

"I think it's going to be very nice around here with her running things," Jack said. "I mean, she always ran a lot of things, but now she'll run everything. She has some very good ideas."

This was not natural. "Doesn't it bother you?" I asked him. "Alida was your *aunt*. As far as I can tell, she cut you out completely."

I don't think Jack realized he should have had expectations of being cut *in*. "Alida didn't cut me out," he said. "I'm director of Literary Services. I've always been director of Literary Services."

"Right," I said.

"We're all getting a raise in salary," Jack said. "Stephen and I, I mean. That was one thing about Alida, you know. She didn't realize what it costs to live these days. She didn't understand."

"Maybe she didn't care," I suggested.

It was not the kind of suggestion Jack welcomed. "Of course she cared," he said. "She had very strict ideas on living and earning a living. Old-fashioned ideas. Good ideas. It's just that she bought her apartment in 1960 and she didn't realize what had happened to rents. Five hundred a month for rent was a lot of money in her day. It was more than the maintenance on her apartment the day she died."

That he didn't believe a word he was saying was obvious. I couldn't understand why he was saying it. Even a compulsive liar lies for effect. I thought of Alida throwing him out of her office, kicking him in the ribs. I considered that fight as a motive for murder. It didn't explain Michael, but I didn't know anything about Michael.

"Fifteen thousand a year was a lot of money in her day, too," Jack said. He gave me another smile. The smile said, "Don't be mad at me. I don't want anyone in the world to be mad at me."

I had to call Phoebe and tell her to call the others. I had to make a list of necessary articles. I had to get my mind on the work I was supposed to do. Jack Brookfield was like a drain clog, something soft and wet cutting off passage.

"Executives don't bring coffee," I told him. "Next time send Janet."

He was impossible to offend. *"She* fired Janet," he said. "We don't have a new receptionist yet."

TWENTY-FOUR

The wardrobe had been moved five inches to the right along the wall. I saw it almost as soon as Jack Brookfield left my office. Putting a paper lampshade on the naked bulb had made the room darker, but it had also got rid of the glare. Between the muted lighting from the ceiling and the indirect from the open door, I could just see the faint outline in the linoleum. That wardrobe must have stood in the same place forever. The outline was less dirt and scuff marks than indentation, and the indentation was deep.

Martinez's people had been over that wardrobe like termites. In the process, they had moved it. That was very sloppy work, and because it was it annoyed me. I sympathized, but it annoyed me. With that naked bulb swinging overhead, it was hard to see *anything.* I had spent the Monday following Michael Brookfield's murder in this room and never noticed anything wrong about the position of the wardrobe. I certainly hadn't noticed any indentations. With half a dozen policemen tramping in and out of a space too small for one, it wasn't surprising Martinez hadn't noticed anything.

If there was anything there to notice.

I tapped my fingernails against the desk and broke one. I could think of two possible explanations. One: the wardrobe had been moved by Martinez or his people during the initial investigation. This would mean the wardrobe had been five inches to the left of where it now stood when Michael Brookfield entered it. There was a hole in the back of that wardrobe, eye-level for a small man. If this theory made any sense, there would be a corresponding hole in the pasteboard wall that divided this room from Martin Lahler's office. Michael Brookfield would have entered the wardrobe in order to look through the hole into that office. This had a certain elegance. Michael Brookfield was cooking his books. Martin Lahler was the firm accountant. Michael was spying on Martin. Fine. But if there was a corresponding hole in the wall of Martin Lahler's office, why hadn't the police found *that?* Or hadn't they been looking?

Two: the wardrobe had been moved since the police investigation, possibly since the last time I had been at Writing Enterprises. This was less elegant. There might be a corresponding hole where the wardrobe was now, which would explain why someone had moved it. It would not, however, explain what Michael had been doing *in* it.

The only way to solve the problem was to move the wardrobe back into its original position. I had a certain amount of ambivalence about that. Hadn't I just been telling myself I wanted out of this investigation? Hadn't I just been doing everything I could think of to get myself out, including starting a fight with the cop in charge?

My ambivalence lasted just long enough. I had hardly managed to convince myself that checking out the wardrobe was a secret act to be committed behind a closed door, meaning it would not commit me to anything, when Stephen Brookfield walked in for a visit.

They weren't going to leave me alone. Alida Brookfield wanted to pretend I wasn't there. Felicity wanted to make me part of the Writing Enterprises Family. Stephen Brookfield didn't say that, but he didn't have to. As soon as I saw what he was carrying under his arm, I knew it.

"I've brought you the cover proof," he told me. "We went through a lot of trouble with this cover. We hired outside talent."

He had the cover proof in his hand. He looked at it upside down, turned it right side up, and put it on my desk. The left half of the board was a mock-up for an ad for a literary agency in Oklahoma. It was headlined $2,000 FOR THE BEST NOVEL! The right half was the result of "outside talent": pink, with lots of hearts, flowers, and curly writing.

I was just ambivalent enough about looking into that wardrobe not to mind the interruption. Stephen Brookfield was just strange enough to make me want that interruption over as soon as possible. He'd looked sick at the morning meeting. Now he looked a skin layer away from being a skeleton. Every time he smiled, he surprised me. I expected a rictus. He gave me Richard Burton in *The Spy Who Came in from the Cold.*

"They didn't give you a chair," he said.

"They gave me the chair I'm sitting on," I said. "Not that it's much of a chair."

He made another Richard Burton smile. The thick stack of papers under his arm quivered and threatened to spill. Unlike Jack, Stephen had no interest in making a good impression, creating an illusion of family unity, or being polite to visitors. He thought I was an inconsequential person, and it showed. I wondered why he had come. Felicity had insisted, I was sure. It didn't seem like enough.

I tried to sit back in my chair like Nero Wolfe considering the evidence. That put the wardrobe directly in my line of vision. I moved. Stephen was not going to leave before he showed me the papers under his arm and said his set piece. Thinking about what I was or wasn't going to do about my wardrobe theories wouldn't make the time go faster. I didn't know what would.

Stephen was eying my desk with a view to sitting on it. He was small and light. It would have been just possible. In the end, he decided not to risk it. He moved to the side, put the papers under his arm in front of me, and backed off. I got the impression he was putting as much distance between us as the space in the office would allow.

"We'll have to give you a visitor's chair," he said. Richard Burton flashed on again. Reluctantly.

Waiting for Stephen to get started was apparently only going to prolong things. Jack could not shut up. When he thought people were looking at him, he filled every silence. Stephen was a journalist's nightmare. He could let silence continue forever. He was waiting for *me*.

"Stephen Brookfield is clean," Martinez had said to me. "He makes fifteen grand a year, he lives in a rattrap, and he's clean. Does that make sense to you?"

It did not make sense to me. A *clean* Stephen Brookfield would not have made sense to me if he made a hundred fifty thousand a year and lived in the Dakota. Stephen Brookfield *oozed*.

I tapped the pile of papers he'd put on my desk. "Am I supposed to look at these?" I asked him. "Are they for the romance section?"

"They're for the romance *line*," he said. "For the Publishing Division." He decided to be magnanimous. "I'm director of Publishing," he explained.

It was going to be like that. "I know you're director of Publishing," I said. "What am I supposed to do with a lot of papers belonging to your romance line? Are you publishing someone I know?"

Stephen Brookfield thought I was being very, very stupid. He also thought I was being willfully recalcitrant. It put him in a bad mood. He didn't want to be here. He wouldn't have wanted to be here even if I were willing to cooperate.

"Felicity thought you'd like to see just how *involved* we are in romance," he said. "She thought if you knew more about us, you'd be less—hostile." That "hostile" was a well-considered word. It was followed by another Richard Burton smile. This one looked genuine. "Felicity," he confided, "doesn't want any trouble right now."

I could have put a hundred connotations on this confession. I would have had to work to take any of them seriously. There had certainly been enough trouble at Writing Enterprises in the last two weeks to make Felicity reluctant to face any more.

"Are these likely to make me less hostile?" I asked Stephen about the papers.

"They're outlines for the next dozen books in the line," Stephen said. "You'll hate them."

"Why?"

"We publish nothing but garbage."

I tried a Phoebe Damereaux eyebrow raise: The Queen Expects to Be Displeased.

"Some people think all romance is garbage," I said. "As a matter of definition."

"We publish *garbage*," Stephen said. "You should see our stable. You should see our books. God, you should see our covers."

"I've seen your covers," I said. "You should use better artists."

"Better artists would cost more money," Stephen said. "Better writers would want royalty agreements."

"You do work-for-hire?"

"We make work-for-hire agreements, yes. Only work-for-hire. That way we can figure the profit without a lot of fuss. Shit, all we're doing is cashing in on the genre market. There's a lot of genre market out there. There're a lot of illiterates out there." This smile was a twist. "It's very appropriate," he said. "I'm an illiterate, too."

"Are you really?"

"More truly than a lot of people know."

I ran my hand through my hair. The conversation was a perpetual motion machine. It was running because it was running. It *kept* running because it was running.

"What's the point of all this?" I asked him. "I thought Felicity wanted this issue done—this section done—in two weeks. How am I supposed to do that if she doesn't leave me alone to work?"

"Maybe it wasn't Felicity," Stephen said. "Maybe I wanted to talk to you."

It was such a blatant lie, it was almost funny. We both looked at each other at once. And giggled.

It broke the barrier. Stephen Brookfield relaxed. It looked as if the bones under his skin had melted. I reached for my cigarettes.

"I might have wanted to talk to you," he said. "It's conceivable."

"About what?" I asked him. "About Writing Enterprises' romance line?"

"God no." He bummed a cigarette. "It was you in the Agenworth case, wasn't it? You're the one who figured it out?"

"Not exactly," I said. Actually, that was *exactly* what I'd done. I had a feeling telling him that would get me in a lot of trouble. "I played a very half-assed role. Sort of."

"Too bad," Stephen said. "If you were into that kind of thing, I could hire you to find out who killed Mike. That'd put a poker up Miss Aldershot's ass."

"That's very interesting," I said. It was, too. Felicity hadn't said as much, but the impression she gave was of complete confidence in the police solution. If the murderer was safely caught and out of the way, there was no reason for life *not* to go on. There was also no reason for the employees of Writing Enterprises not to put the good of the company first.

"I take it you don't think Ivy Samuels did it," I said.

"Felicity thinks Ivy Samuels did it," Stephen said.

"She's the only one?"

"Even she only wants to think it. They're saying Mike tried to blackmail this woman. Michael couldn't blackmail anybody."

"He was short of cash," I said. "He had an expensive girlfriend."

"Yeah," Stephen said. "So he cooked his books. He was crazy over that female, no question. But Michael was like Jack, you know. He couldn't do anything so illegal he'd have to know it was illegal."

"He didn't know embezzling was illegal?"

"He didn't look on it as embezzling. He had explanations." Stephen shook his head. "Look at Jack," he said. "Jack steals the milk money—you know, postage cash, petty cash, loose funds. You'd be amazed how much you can make doing that. He's supposed to go take some money out of the bank, he takes a little more than he says he did. Business money. You could talk yourself into a lunatic asylum and not convince him he was stealing. He's got explanations."

"I'd like to hear some of them," I said.

"They're nonsense," Stephen said, "but Jack's got a whole rationale worked out so *he* doesn't think they're nonsense. That's the point. I don't think you could stretch those kinds of rationalizations far enough to cover blackmail."

"I don't see how you could stretch them to cover embezzling."

"People do it all the time. They're just borrowing. Michael had it easier than most people in his position. He was related to the boss."

"And thought he would inherit?" I ventured.

"Now, now," Stephen said. "Actually, we all knew we weren't inheriting anything. Alida wasn't keeping it secret. We didn't know Felicity had her position nailed down so—solidly—but we knew we weren't getting anything. Oddly enough, it's working out better than I'd have expected."

"Oddly enough?"

"Jack was right," Stephen said. "Nobody's talking about firing anybody. That's some kind of miracle." He stubbed his cigarette out, shoved his hands in his pockets, and looked around. "I guess I'd better get out of here," he said. He actually sounded reluctant. "I've taken up enough time to say my piece. Felicity will want a report."

"You can tell her we got on famously," I said.

"I just won't tell her why." He started out the door. He hadn't made it into the hall before he stopped, turned around, and came back.

"Let me give you these," he said, starting to fiddle with something in his back pants pockets. He threw a couple of thin paperback books on my desk, fiddled some more, and came up with another one. "The Amorous Adventure Line from Writing Enterprises," he laughed. "Have fun."

"I will," I said.

I waited till I heard his footsteps moving away in the corridor. Then I shoved the three romance books into my bag, got up, and headed for the wardrobe again. I was going to have to work out what had changed between Stephen and me, and why, and how, but I could do that later. Right now, I wanted to move that wardrobe.

I didn't have a chance. I was just closing the door to the corridor when the Art Director knocked on it.

He was carrying mechanicals.

TWENTY-FIVE

"It was like that all day," I told Phoebe when I got her into McGrath's that night. "It was a screenplay. Felicity had them all lined up. They came to see me one by one. They all had speeches." I corrected this. "Monologues," I said. "Except for Stephen Brookfield, all I got was monologues. If I broke in, I got slightly shifted monologues. The general idea was everything in the Brookfield family was much better than it looked."

"Was it?" Phoebe asked.

"How the hell should I know?" I signaled to the bartender for another Drambuie straight up and started searching my bag for cigarettes. "The problem," I said, "is that I just don't know if I want to be involved in this thing. If I get shoved into it, I can't help myself. When I have half a second to think, I want to go to Connecticut for the weekend."

"Existential angst," Phoebe said. "You were always prone to it."

"I'm not prone to existential angst," I said. "I just don't know what I'm doing."

Phoebe sipped at her champagne. It was very bad champagne, very sweet and very pink. Her favorite kind.

"I know what you should be doing," she said. "You should be calling up Martinez and explaining about the wardrobe."

It took a large swallow of Drambuie to keep me from groaning out loud. I had been at Writing Enterprises until almost six o'clock, after having been subjected for over eight hours to a near-constant stream of inane conversation. I'd called Phoebe because she was the one person who could always calm me down, if she wanted to. Even in college she could calm me down, and I spent most of my college career trying to decide if I wanted to go interestingly psychotic or become a violent revolutionary.

Apparently, Phoebe did not want to calm me down. She sat on her high bar stool, feet dangling over the floor, and looked determined. She also looked stubborn. Phoebe has a great many admirable qualities and a few not-so-admirable ones. As with most people, some of those qualities are more in evidence than others at any particular time. She is, however, always stubborn and determined.

At the moment, she was stubbornly determined to get "us" involved in the Brookfield murders. Since the only way "we" could be involved was if I were involved, she wanted to have done with what she termed my "Hamlet thing."

"Martinez could go in and move that wardrobe," she said.

"Martinez has his case," I reminded her. "Why would he want something that might jeopardize it?"

"You underrate him."

"You overrate him."

"Finding out about the wardrobe was what he asked you to do," she said. "You did it. Call him up and tell him."

I sighed and stared into my glass. "The last time," I said, "I was accused of a murder and I had to do something. There's no reason for doing anything this time. Nick doesn't think Ivy will be convicted. I've got no interest in the Brookfields. God only knows, if I could think of a way never to go back to that office, I'd take it."

Phoebe tapped the edge of her glass. "It won't be the same this time as before," she said. "You don't know those people. You can be objective. It won't matter so much when they catch—whoever."

"I'll have to testify at the trial."

"It won't matter so much," Phoebe insisted.

I said, "I suppose not," and concentrated on my drink. Phoebe played with the swizzle stick I'd put aside and ruminated.

"The problem," she said, "is you've got four people, any one of whom might have committed two murders." She paused. "Maybe five," she said. She paused again. "Maybe six. I'm adding Mrs. Haskell and Janet."

"Felicity Aldershot fired Janet," I said. "Maybe Felicity knows Janet killed them and doesn't want the girl around."

Phoebe brightened. I was finally Cooperating. "Exactly," she said. "I mean, I don't think that's what really happened, you understand, but—well, we'll put Mrs. Haskell and Janet to one side and concentrate on the others, but we'll remember Mrs. Haskell and Janet are *there*."

"The others, meaning Felicity, Stephen, Jack, and Ivy."

"No, no, no," Phoebe said. "Felicity, Stephen, Jack, and that *accountant*."

"Martin Lahler?"

"Why not?"

"You don't know Martin Lahler," I said. I thought of that scene in the Russian Tea Room. "In the first place, he's not very intelligent. In the second place, he's a coward. Physical and moral. Phoebe, if you're going to look at this as a puzzle, you're going to have to at least start with the assumption that everything fits. You've got two people dead and no determining physical evidence of who killed them. That is not the result of stupidity."

"It could have been an accident," Phoebe said.

"An accident that both times everybody with any possible motive was wandering around Writing Enterprises—wandering, so nobody has an alibi—including two people who didn't work there and had no reason as far as anyone knew to be expected there—stop," I said.

"Stop what?" Phoebe said.

"That's the key. Don't put Mrs. Haskell and Janet to one side. Put Mrs. Haskell and Ivy to one side."

"What are you talking about?"

"Mrs. Haskell and Ivy. They're both outsiders. I don't know why Mrs. Haskell showed up when she did, but Ivy showed up because she'd been contacted. Once by letter and once by phone. She didn't have a motive until she was contacted, either. She didn't exactly have one *after* she was contacted, but there was the inference, and in the event the inference was enough. Now—oh, hell," I said. I grabbed my bag and started pawing through it. "I need a pen." I pulled out my checkbook and my card case. I pulled out the three romance novels Stephen Brookfield had given me. I pulled out one of Camille's defunct flea collars. "We've got to write it all down," I said. I found a pen.

I got up, leaned over the bar, and took a wad of napkins. "Mrs. Haskell and Ivy," I said, writing their names on one side of the napkin, "and then on the other side the Brookfields and Felicity Aldershot. I'll put Martin in for the sake of form. Now look, we make a list of everything that happened. Then we make a list of what we know about the people it happened to. Then—" I was running out of space. I pushed the mess I'd taken from my purse to one side. I opened another napkin. "I'll make headings for everything," I said. "Then we'll fill in the blanks. We'll treat it like one of those logic puzzles. You know, Mr. Green lives in the red house and the man who lives in the green house is not the carpenter."

"You're going to dump that stuff on the floor," Phoebe said.

"I'll pick it up in a minute," I said. "The first thing is Events. Under Events we put only those things we actually know happened. Not things people told us, or assumed, or—damn." I pushed the mess one more time. "Under information," I started.

The card case clattered when it hit the floor. The rest of the stuff made a sound like dying leaves. I jumped down to pick it up, distracted, and shoved it onto the bar.

"We'll have to make a list of what people told us," I was saying as I climbed back onto my seat, "and who told us what, so we can figure out—what's the matter?"

Phoebe had lost all interest in treating the Brookfield murders as a puzzle. She was turning something over and over in her hands. She looked very worried.

"Patience," she asked me, "have you been feeling all right?"

"You know how I've been feeling. Etzy-ketzy, as Nick would say."

"You've been losing a lot of weight, haven't you?"

"What's the matter with you?" I asked her. I grabbed the thing in her hands. "You look like a relative died," I said.

Then I opened my hand and looked down at a small glassine envelope full of white powder.

TWENTY-SIX

It was Stephen Brookfield's. I knew that as soon as I saw it. It explained a lot of things: the emaciation, the air of being the chief character in a novel about expatriate dissolutes, the pallor, the sudden laughing fit. I had once heard Alida tell Jack she knew "what he was doing in the men's room," but Alida frequently got things mixed up. Jack Brookfield could not be a drug addict. No drug addict is ever that fat. Stephen Brookfield not only could be, he probably was. Assuming what I had in my hands was dope.

Assuming what I had in my hands was dope? I looked at the glassine envelope again. It looked exactly like the glassine envelopes that figured so prominently in syndicated reruns of "The Streets of San Francisco." For all I knew about dope, it could have been castor sugar. Or Bromo-Seltzer. Or nitroglycerin, for that matter. I didn't have the faintest idea what nitroglycerin looked like.

Neither, apparently, did Phoebe. Having recovered from her shock at finding it among my things and her relief at realizing it wasn't mine, she was as much in need of a solid identification as I was.

"Martinez will know," she said.

I shook my head. "I don't want to go to Martinez," I said. "I'd have to tell him where I got it."

"Do you know where you got it?"

I nodded. "It had to be in one of the romance books," I said. "It must have been in Stephen Brookfield's back pocket and so were the romance books and when he took the romance books out it got stuck."

"I thought you didn't like Stephen Brookfield."

"He's creepy. Like the mummy in a fifties horror movie. But I don't hate him."

"Patience—" Phoebe said.

"Don't call me Patience," I said. "We don't know this has anything to do with the murders. You should see this guy, Phoebe. He's a skeleton. He's probably been using a long time. If he's using."

"*You* think he's using," Phoebe said.

"Yes, I do. That doesn't mean I have to turn him into the police."

Phoebe threw her hands in the air. "What do you *want* to do, McKenna? Snort it and see if you get high?"

"Do you snort heroin?"

"Oh, for God's sake."

I put the envelope into my pocket out of sight. I didn't want the bartender seeing it. Maybe I didn't want anyone seeing it. On the other hand, I didn't want to "snort it and see if I got high," either.

"Just maybe," Phoebe said, "something that has to do with that bag is what made him kill two people. You said they didn't make much money. It takes a lot of money to support a habit. At least, according to the newspapers it does. Your Stephen Brookfield could have been robbing the company blind, he could have been robbing Alida Brookfield's private funds. He could have—"

"He wasn't," I said. "Martinez told me that. They did an audit as part of the investigation. They didn't come up with anything financial on Stephen. Matinez told me so."

"Stop repeating 'Martinez told me so,'" Phoebe said. "And an audit wouldn't come up with everything. He could be selling off supplies. Or getting kickbacks. Or *something*."

"All right," I said. "All right, all right."

"And if he's clean," Phoebe said. "Pay, for God's sake. If he *is* clean, that's *weirder*."

"It's not just weirder, it's impossible," I said. I put my head in my hands and tried to think. I didn't want to go to Martinez, not yet. We had not been friendly last time we met, and I didn't think things were going to get any friendlier soon. I didn't want to get Stephen in trouble just because he had a drug habit. I can be very moralistic about drugs, but I'm reluctant to make it official.

"We've got to find out for certain what this is," I said. "That's the immediate problem, right?"

"Right," Phoebe said. She was deliberately imitating me, but I ignored her.

"Let's go talk to Nick," I said.

"Would Nick *know?*" Phoebe asked.

"How do I know if he'd know? He might know somebody who would know."

"In the movies they taste it," Phoebe said.

I got a wad of money out of my wallet and threw two singles on the bar. One of the advantages of frequenting low-life bars is that they always make you pay when served.

"I'm going out to get a cab," I said.

Phoebe was ahead of me. By the time I straggled out to Columbus Avenue, she had one waiting.

TWENTY-SEVEN

Scene from an Ingmar Bergman movie: Three people circling a coffee table. One of them points to an object on the table. Another shakes his head. A third bites her fingernails. Everybody sits down and looks suicidal, or at least hopeless.

It went on like that for an hour. Nick's apartment is in the Village, on a quiet residential street protected by trees and distance from the commercial circus of Sixth Avenue and Bleecker. He has two rooms and a kitchen. His coffee table had to have been stolen from the Sunday morning garbage outside an East Side high-rise. None of this helped us determine whether or not what was in that glassine envelope was heroin.

"I could taste it," he said.

I pointed out the suggestion had been made before. "Besides," I said, "aren't they always cutting it with bicarbonate of soda? Why wouldn't it taste just like bicarbonate of soda?"

"I shouldn't have it here at all," Nick said. "I'm supposed to be an officer of the court."

"Don't sound like Daniel Harte."

"Daniel Harte," Nick said. "Daniel Harte got bounced from Cravath."

This was the first good news either of us had had all day. We went with it.

"My opinion of Cravath went way up," Nick said. "If they had sense enough to fire the guy, they can't be complete idiots."

"They should have had sense enough not to hire him," I said.

"You know what these places are," Nick said. "He was on the law review."

"You were on the law review," I said.

"This isn't getting us anywhere," Phoebe said.

Nick and I stopped, and blushed, and stared at our hands. Then we both got up and started pacing. It was very depressing. A year ago, nothing would have stopped us, not even violence. Now we needed extraordinary circumstances just to get started. I had good reason to be ambivalent about getting involved in a murder case. The last time I'd been involved in a murder case, it had changed everything. Contrary to the assumption that allowed me to indulge in periodic orgies of self-conscious guilt, not *all* the changes had been for the better.

"I think the question here," Phoebe said, "is whether or not we're looking at a Baggie full of heroin."

"It's not a Baggie," Nick said. "It's a tiny plastic bag. A Baggie full of heroin could set you up for life."

"It could be cocaine," Phoebe said.

I stopped pacing to paw through my bag, hunting cigarettes. I came up with the three Writing Enterprises romance novels and threw them on the table near the envelope.

"They ought to be arrested for what they do to writers," I said. "They ought to be stopped, anyway."

Phoebe sniffed. "Something like this ought to put a crimp in their business," she said.

While she was saying this I was holding a match to my cigarette. I laughed. I inhaled a lung full of sulfur.

"Shit," I said, meaning not only the sulfur but her suppositions. "You ought to go down there. It's like none of this ever happened. Felicity Aldershot is playing Chairwoman of the Board and the rest of them are running around trying to figure out how to keep doing what they've been doing. Worse, they're trying to think of how to expand."

"How could they expand?" Phoebe said. "What would they expand into?"

"The international market plus one," I said. "Felicity Aldershot took me to lunch. That's in keeping with her policy, formulated sometime in my absence, that I am to be Kept Happy. Or busy, to be more accurate."

"Can you get this done in a week?" Nick said. "Is it possible?"

"If everything goes right and she gives me time to do the work," I said. "If the articles come in by Saturday and I've got them edited by Monday, we ought to be ready for the printer sometime next Friday, everybody working overtime. Except the printer, because that's the point. The printer isn't supposed to work overtime. The staff gets paid straight salary so they don't get extra for overtime."

"Don't get much straight salary, either, from what I heard," Phoebe said.

"We've been over this before," I said. "I'm not getting anything done if Felicity Aldershot keeps taking me to lunch. A two-hour lunch, mind you. At the Oyster Bar, which is halfway up-town. A two-hour lunch with an extra half hour in cabs."

"To tell you they're expanding?" Nick said.

"Writing Workshops and Correspondence Schools is ex-panding," I said. "Overseas. That's Felicity's big new idea. They're going to hold summer writers' conferences in Europe. Greece, to start with."

"A writer's conference in Greece?" Nick said. "The Greeks don't read any books. They read fewer books per capita than any other country in Europe."

"Think of Sophocles," I said. "Think of Homer."

"Think of the piracy," Nick said. "I did a case for—what's her name—Joan Liddell? The romantic suspense lady. Anyway, they pirate everything, the Greeks. They have unauthorized editions out before the authorized ones get into the country, they reprint verbatim in newspapers. You can't sell anything over there. It's a nightmare."

"It's a chance to charge a lot of money for very little service," I said. "The tuition alone is going to be three times what they ask for a conference in San Diego or Houston. And that doesn't count transportation, or room and board fees, or incidentals like registration and reservation charges. They're going to make a mint."

"It's going to work?"

"Of course it's going to work." I snatched the books from the table and dumped them on the floor. "You know why I don't want to turn Stephen Brookfield in? He's at least honest about it. He's in a racket and he knows he's in a racket and he doesn't try to pretend it's something nice and respectable."

"That sounds—amoral," Nick said. "It's the kind of thing a DA would try to prove when he wanted to call someone a hard-ened criminal."

"Call Felicity Aldershot a hardened criminal," I said. "Or Jack Brookfield. I go nuts every time I talk to either of those two. Jack wants you to punish him. He practically lies down and begs for it. Felicity thinks everything is a problem in applied economics."

"This isn't getting us anywhere," Phoebe said.

I started toward the kitchen. "Maybe I don't want to get anywhere," I said. "Give me an excuse to get the other two arrested and I'll want to get somewhere."

"Plant this stuff on them," Nick said. "Warn Stephen Brookfield. Call a cop and start a bust."

I took the kettle off the stove, filled it with water, put it back on again, and turned on the gas. Out in the living room, Phoebe said, "This isn't getting us anywhere" for the third time.

Nick said, "What do you want from me? I don't *have* a lot of strange friends with offices in Times Square basements and back rooms full of chemistry sets."

"You must know *someone*," Phoebe said.

The phone started ringing. I got coffee from the shelf over the sink, put it on the counter, and crossed the room to answer it. I knew Nick's apartment well: phones in the kitchen and the bedroom, no answering machines.

Martinez recognized my voice and said, "It's you."

I started searching my pockets for my cigarettes. They were in the living room.

"Nick's here," I said. "I'll get him."

"Yeah," Martinez said. "Get him. There's been a little trouble out here."

TWENTY-EIGHT

Her name was Irene Joan Haskell and she had—literally—been beaten to a pulp. "Face and neck," Martinez said when we got there. "Baseball bat." "There" was a lower-middle-class neighborhood in Brooklyn, one of those streets where the brownstones have wide squat stoops and the corner store sells sausage grinders and New York's Best Pizza. Irene Joan Haskell lived almost midway down the block, on the north side. She was gone by the time we got there. What was left was a series of small pools of blood on each of the four top steps of the stoop. It was very cold. A custard skin of ice was forming on each of the pools. Ice was forming on the hands of Ivy Samuels Tree, too. She didn't seem able to move.

"Not dead," Martinez said when Nick asked him about Mrs. Haskell. "Unconscious, yes. Close, yes. But not dead."

"Jesus Christ," Nick said.

"I wouldn't even have known about it," Martinez said. "They put Mrs. Tree's name in the computer. They got me."

"Yeah," Nick said. "They would."

"I came right away." Martinez turned to look at Ivy, sitting motionless on the steps of the brownstone next door to Irene Haskell's, surrounded by four uniformed patrolmen. Her arms were hanging at her sides. Her eyes were staring into space. "She says she was called," Martinez said. "She's always saying she was called."

He turned his back on us. Nick and I stood silently for a moment, watching him walk away. It was dark. The police floodlights only made it look darker still. There were lights in every window, up and down the street. There were people behind every curtain.

"We have to talk to her," Nick said. He said it the way he'd say "grass is green"—as if it were a statement that anticipated no action.

I pointed across the street. "Phoebe's talking to her," I said. Phoebe had pushed through the cordon of police and sat down beside Ivy. Ivy hadn't noticed her. "Maybe Phoebe can get things started," I said.

It sounded lame, and it was. Nick's head started shaking in an oddly involuntary swing. "Beaten with a baseball bat," he said. "At least the other two were strangled. That's not a wonderful way to die, but they didn't suffer *long*. But beaten with a baseball bat, for God's sake. She must have screamed."

"She screamed," I said. "Martinez said that. She screamed and someone in the apartments around her called the police."

"That's nice," Nick said.

There was no answer to that. I put my hands in the pockets of my coat to get them warm and rocked back and forth on the balls of my feet. The temperature had to be well below freezing. The wind was very strong. Across the street, Phoebe put her arms around Ivy's shoulders and patted her.

"They'll get a conviction after this," Nick said. "I don't think she killed those two people and I don't think Martinez thinks so either, but they'll get a conviction after this. Even if we don't let them introduce the pictures."

I wanted to smoke, but I didn't want my hands exposed to the air. "We ought to talk to her," I said. "She told Martinez she was called. Nick—"

"Don't," Nick said. "Don't say it."

"It's relevant."

"It's not relevant to me. It worked last time, I admit it, but I didn't approve of it. And even now I don't think it was necessary."

"I'm not talking about something that worked," I said. "I'm talking about something that is." I started flapping around in the air, trying to get warm, trying to think. Too much had been happening too fast. I was emotionally numb and mentally dull. The landscape didn't help. This neighborhood didn't look like New York at all. It looked like a small industrial city in Pennsylvania, one week before the factories started moving out.

"Two things," I said. "In the first place, she was called. Somebody's trying to set her up. Maybe someone has been trying to set her up all along. That first letter—"

"Was written by Michael Brookfield, who is dead."

"Written by Michael Brookfield," I said. "Maybe not inspired by Michael Brookfield. And it didn't mention blackmail, you know. It didn't even hint at it."

"Dortman and Hodges suspended her contract," Nick said. "We can't even get them for race discrimination. They can say they did it because of the murders."

"Stephen said Michael was like Jack," I said. "Eager to please. He could have sent that letter because someone suggested he send that letter."

"Find the someone who suggested the letter. Prove they suggested it."

"She had no reason to hurt Irene Haskell," I said. "The only thing Irene Haskell's done recently to cause trouble for someone is—" I stopped. "Wait a minute," I said. "The audit. She threatened an audit."

"You have audits on the brain," Nick said. "Last time it was an audit. This time you want an audit, too."

"But it hooks up with Michael Brookfield," I said. "Michael Brookfield was embezzling."

"Michael Brookfield is dead," Nick said. "He couldn't have bashed up Mrs. Haskell for asking for an audit that might reveal his embezzling. Never mind the fact his embezzling had already been revealed."

"Michael Brookfield was embezzling," I said, "which could have caused an audit."

Nick ran his hands through his hair. "Difficulties," he said. "You're always causing difficulties. You want me to tell you how to get out of these difficulties? You want the simplest explanation?"

"Nick," I said.

"Don't 'Nick' me," he said. "Look at it this way. Two people dead. Both times, Irene Haskell accidentally on the scene. Ivy knows Mrs. Haskell knows something, anything. Maybe Mrs. Haskell even calls and says she knows something. Superfluous. Ivy—"

"Do you think Ivy did it?"

"I think they'd better be right when they say Harvard's the best law school in the country," Nick said. "I'm going to need something going for me."

• • •

He had nothing going for him, and neither did I. We didn't even have Ivy.

Phoebe stood up when she saw us cross the street, patted Ivy once more on the shoulder, and gave us an exaggerated shrug. As far as anyone could tell, Ivy had never known Phoebe was there. She hadn't moved. She hadn't spoken. When they made the formal arrest, she gave no indication she knew what they were doing. She went docilely enough when a uniformed patrolman took her arm to guide her to a police car, but she looked like an automaton.

She was booked somewhere in Brooklyn, in a large, dingy building that looked as if it might once have been a prison, or a meat-packing house. It was completely deserted. We stood in a knot in the center of a large room and watched them fingerprint Ivy. They'd have aroused more emotion in a wooden Indian. Ivy made them very, very nervous.

"Ambulance," Tony Marsh said. Martinez had brought Tony with him. Martinez's regular partner—a nonentity whose face I could never remember and whose name I had never known—was off duty and temporarily out of contact. It was against regulations to be out of contact. Martinez was usually very big on regulations. This time he didn't seem to mind.

"We ought to get her to a hospital," Tony Marsh said. "She's outta her head. She isn't *seeing* anything."

"It's just shock," I said. "Emotional shock. She needs some tea and a shot of brandy and a long rest."

"Sugar's good for shock," Tony Marsh said. Then he gave me an odd look. "Don't you want her to go to the hospital? I thought she was a friend of yours."

Second time, I thought. This time I didn't go into an explanation of how and why I'd met Ivy Samuels Tree. I said, "They won't let her go into the hospital. Not unless Nick gets a judge and the judge makes them. Extreme emotional disturbance."

Tony Marsh grunted. Extreme emotional disturbance is a legal defense in murder cases in the state of New York. It means exactly what it says. If you were a victim of extreme emotional disturbance at the time you committed a murder, you can't be convicted of it. That was the law that got Richard Herrin off in the Bonnie Garland case—after he'd caved her head in with a hammer.

"I came over to tell you the lieutenant wanted to talk to you," Tony Marsh said. Then, as if this weren't enough, "I guess I ought to tell you."

I looked around for Martinez. He had taken a seat at an empty metal desk in the far corner of the room. He was smoking a cigarette and tapping his fingers against the armrests of his chair. When he saw me looking at him he nodded and motioned me to him.

I went. I didn't hurry. Martinez had not only given me no indication we were back on friendly terms, since I left him at the Lincoln Square Coffee Shoppe he had yet to say hello to me. Of course, Nick wasn't happy with me either, so staying close to the knot of people around Ivy wasn't much safer than crossing the room to talk to Martinez. I wound my way through the desks, running my hands across their tops like a kid running a stick down a picket fence.

"Can't talk to him," Martinez said when I got to his corner. He made a jerking head motion at Nick. "They wouldn't love me for talking to the defense attorney. Have to talk to you."

I got a chair from a nearby desk, dragged it over, and sat down in it.

"You think she's some kind of nutcase?" Martinez asked me.

"I don't know her," I said. "From the few times I've talked to her, I wouldn't have thought so."

"Do you know what she did?" Martinez asked. "Only a nutcase could do what she did. She stayed there, for Christ's sake."

"Stayed there?"

"She was there when the officers got there. Walking up and down those stairs. Picking up that goddamned baseball bat. She was just wandering around."

"Like that?" I motioned to the other side of the room.

"Almost," Martinez said. "Not quite so bad. She told us she'd got a phone call. Said this woman introduced herself as Martha Haskell—" Martinez blinked. "*Martha* Haskell," he repeated.

"She *was* set up," I said.

Martinez shrugged. "Or she came on her own, without any phone call. Didn't know the woman's name."

"All right," I said.

Martinez was still kicking it around. He came to some decision, sealed it by straightening his tie, and said, "What she told us. Some woman called and said she was Martha Haskell. Said she knew Mrs. Tree was being framed. Said she could prove it and would prove it only Mrs. Tree had to see her right away. So Mrs. Tree, being one of Nick Carras's standard criminal clients, got herself on a train and came to New York. Without calling her lawyer for advice. Naturally." Martinez made an attempt at what could only have been a smile. "You never asked for advice either," he said.

I didn't want to talk about myself. "Did she tell—whoever it was—that she had to take a train? Did she say anything about how long it would take her to get here?"

"I don't know. She got—like that—before we had a chance to ask any questions. Hell, by the time I got on the scene, she *was* like that. I'm only telling you what the officers told me."

"That she said she'd been called."

"Exactly."

I gave him my best journalist's search. There was nothing to see in his face.

"Do you think she did it?" I asked him. "Do you think she killed two people and bludgeoned a third one into a coma?"

"I arrested her the first time," he said. "I would have arrested her for this."

"That doesn't tell me anything."

"Intelligent of you to realize it."

I got out my cigarettes and, finally, lit one. It felt like hours since I'd had any nicotine. Maybe it had been hours. I had no idea how long we'd stood in the cold on that Brooklyn street.

I wanted to ask him if he *had* set me up, if he'd wanted to arrest Ivy all the time and fed me information meant to distract my attention from the true course of the investigation. I couldn't. It felt too good just to be talking to him again.

"Is this what you wanted me to tell Nick?" I asked him. "That she said she'd been called, by *Martha* Haskell?"

"I wanted you to tell him the facts," Martinez said. "The fact that she was found standing over the body with that baseball bat in her hand. The fact that the blood was fresh. The fact that we aren't going to be able to let her out on bail this time."

"Can she be denied bail? On an assault charge?"

"If I work at it."

"And you're going to work at it."

"Yeah," Martinez said. "I have to work at it. If I don't work at it, someone's going to have my head."

We both looked across the room at Ivy. They had finished taking her fingerprints. They had washed her hands and folded them in her lap. She was sitting motionless, oblivious.

While we were looking at her she raised her head, stared at no one and nothing in particular, and said, "Maybe I'm sleepwalking. Maybe I'm doing it in my sleep."

TWENTY-NINE

Police wisdom: it is easier to find something if you know what you're looking for. It is impossible *not* to find something if you know exactly what you're looking for.

I knew what I was looking for. I needed something Michael Brookfield, Alida Brookfield, and Irene Haskell had in common, beyond the fact that all of them had been victims of violence. I needed other things as well, but they could wait until later. *Why*, for instance. I would have liked to know why whatever it was they had in common *made* them candidates for violence.

Unfortunately, what I was looking for did not seem "impossible not to find" or even "easy." Nor was the situation helped by Phoebe's determination to play Nancy Drew and Nick's to play ostrich. Nick not only wanted to play ostrich, he wanted everyone to play ostrich with him.

"We've been over this before," he said, when I finally got him out of Brooklyn and into my apartment. "Interested parties in a murder case shouldn't run around investigating on their own. It gets them into trouble, not out of it."

"It got me out of it."

"Not until after you'd been arrested for second-degree murder, it didn't. And you'd never have been arrested in the first place if you'd kept your nose out of it."

"That isn't true and you know it."

"I don't know what I know."

I gave him a shot of whiskey and put him to bed with my best down comforter. He got into bed wearing jockey shorts, warm-up pants, three pairs of socks, and a zip-up Harvard sweatshirt. Nick is very serious about No Sex Without Commitment. Proximity, being dangerous, can be tolerated only under conditions of maximum preparedness.

I waited until he was safely settled with a copy of the latest David Halberstam exposé (in hardcover—Nick carries David Halberstam hardcovers in his briefcase) and went to the kitchen to phone Phoebe.

Phoebe, being Phoebe, was up. Phoebe is *always* up.

"I've started on those lists you mentioned," she said. "You know, Events. And Suppositions."

"Forget about the lists for a minute," I said. "I want to know something. How many people knew about Ivy?"

"How many people knew what about Ivy?"

"That she was black. That someone was going to a lot of trouble not to let the general public know she was black."

"Everybody," Phoebe said.

"Everybody?"

"You know what I mean. It was an open secret. Even the contract was an open secret, really. Hazel knew about it."

Hazel Ganz was a category romance writer and rights officer of the American Writers of Romance.

"That contract sucks," I said. "I can't see Hazel letting it go. It's just the kind of thing she likes to start a fight over."

"Hazel had to let it go," Phoebe said. "She couldn't do anything about it unless Ivy wanted to do something about it, and Ivy couldn't do anything about it because she couldn't afford to, so—"

"So," I said. "Never mind. It doesn't matter. If 'everybody' knew about it, it wouldn't have been hard for someone at Writing Enterprises to find out about it. It probably just came up."

"Probably," Phoebe said. "So what?"

"So what," I repeated. "The ultimate question. What did Janine used to say? If you haven't got an answer, you haven't got a book."

"Let's not talk about Janine," Phoebe said.

"No," I agreed. "Let's not talk about Janine. I was just hoping it was difficult to get that information. So we could trace how it got to Writing Enterprises. It could have given us a handle."

"Are you reading Nero Wolfe again?"

"Jack Webb. Never mind. Go to sleep."

"Eat something," Phoebe said. "Then go to sleep yourself."

I dreamed of a Writer's Conference, set on a hill. Everyone was there. Even people who'd been dead more than a year were there. Myrra gave a lecture on The Art of Love. Phoebe gave one on The *Act* of Love and illustrated it with diagrams projected on a screen. People came in one end, wandered through miles of alleys past a confusing conglomeration of exhibits, and wandered out into the arms of Alida Brookfield. Alida Brookfield had a sign on her forehead that said HOW TO GET PUBLISHED THE EASY WAY. She had very large, sharp teeth.

I got up and looked at the alarm clock. Quarter to five. I turned off the alarm and put it under the bed. Once I'm awake, I'm awake for hours, no matter how little sleep I've had. Even when I've been drinking, I can't close my eyes after opening them and get them to stay closed. I got out of bed and headed for the kitchen, not bothering to be careful not to wake Nick. It is not possible to wake Nick.

There was nothing in my refrigerator but a quarter pound of butter, a pint of Devon cream, and some leftover take-out Chinese from last Thursday. I threw out the Chinese. I looked in the wooden breadbox Phoebe had given me for my birthday (hope springs eternal) and found a loaf of whole wheat, moldy, and half a dozen bagels, stale. I looked into the refrigerator again. The cream cheese was in the freezer. I took it out. I started the oven. I cut two of the bagels in half, threw water on them, and put them in the oven to de-stale. Then I started the coffee.

"Hundred and nine," I said. "No wonder I weigh a hundred and nine." I reached down to scratch the cat. Camille was weaving in and out of my legs. If *my* breakfast was going to be early, *her* breakfast was going to be early.

"Too many characters in this play," I said.

I stopped. Camille butted her head against my hand. Scratching was not supposed to stop until she wanted it to stop. I picked her up and put her in my lap.

"Not too many characters in this play," I said. "Six. That's the point."

There were pencils and pads on the sideboard. I leaned over and got one of each. I wrote:

Michael Brookfield——girlfriend——embezzling
Jack Brookfield——stock market?——stealing
Stephen Brookfield——heroin?——?
Felicity Aldershot——ambition——takes over everyone's
                        job, makes sure A.B. knows it

Alida Brookfield——money——anything she can think of
Martin Lahler——?——?

I considered this list, then divided it into subsets. I put Michael
and Alida to one side. I put Jack, Stephen, Felicity Aldershot,
and Martin Lahler to the other. On the bottom of the page I
wrote: *Irene Haskell, Ivy.*

In a terrible way, the attack on Irene Haskell simplified things.
Until that happened, she could, possibly, have figured as a suspect. As a victim, she was of interest to the people at Writing
Enterprises for one reason only. She was going to sue them. She
was going to attach their business records and force an audit.
One of those four—Stephen, Jack, Felicity, Martin—didn't want
those records attached.

The obvious suspect was Martin. Fiddling accountants are a
capitalist cliché. Besides, Martin was the only one not solidly
connected. Stephen and Jack were family. Felicity Aldershot,
from what I had seen of her relationship with Alida, was *better*
than family.

Martin Lahler didn't interest me for the moment, however. It
was Stephen Brookfield I wanted to talk to.

Stephen and a receptionist named Janet.

THIRTY

No one at Writing Enterprises had heard about the attack on
Irene Haskell. I should have expected it, but I didn't. I had spent
so much of the night thinking about Ivy, talking about Ivy, deal-
ing with Ivy—and so little of it asleep—it would have surprised
me if my dry cleaner hadn't heard about it.

Writing Enterprises was in the grip of a New Enthusiasm. Felicity Aldershot actually called it that, as if she were the PR woman for a children's camp. The reception area, still minus receptionist, was filled with large pieces of posterboard. Hijacked Art Department assistants were bending over the posterboard, drawing schematic designs for everything from a new cover logo to a new table of contents format. *Writing: The Magazine for Professional Freelancers* was getting a face-lift.

"Image is so important," Felicity said, when she caught me emerging from the elevator. "Alida could never understand that. People look at your product and *feel* you're first class—or they don't."

"Is this new enthusiasm going to extend to the articles?" I asked her. "Are you going to start suggesting honest research and New York agents?"

"The purpose of a magazine," Felicity said, "is to deliver its readers to its advertisers."

This was conventional magazine-publishing wisdom. People who own magazines actually believe it. I didn't think it meant anything in this case. I said so.

"It means exactly what it says," Felicity told me. "I know my advertisers. I know what they want from me and the readers they want to see me deliver. This is not *Sophistication*. This is not an upmarket publication. We're read by the failures of this world, Miss McKenna, and we give them hope."

I could have untangled this logic if I tried. I didn't.

"Actually," Felicity Aldershot was saying, "we're getting a lot more militant. I've got an article on my desk—it came in last week but I just got to it this morning—on how to manage subsidy publishing."

"Subsidy publishing? You mean a vanity press?"

"It's the only way some of these people are going to get into print," Felicity Aldershot said.

"It doesn't count," I said.

"Quite a few very successful writers started out printing their own books," she said.

"Not lately. Lately, the only self-published book I can remember getting any real press was *On a Clear Day You Can See General Motors.* And that was by an experienced writer, who started with a contract from Playboy Press, and the reason it ended up self-published had to do with *legal* questions. And he didn't put it out through a vanity press, either."

"They want to impress their friends and relatives," Felicity Aldershot said. "Their friends and relatives won't know the difference."

"They get told they're going to make a lot of money," I said. "They *don't* get told the bookstores won't handle their books and the reviewers won't read them, never mind review them, and—"

"Didn't you say there was something you wanted to talk to me about?"

It was a good move. I'd come in intending to find out what she knew about Irene Haskell. I'd forgotten all about it. Now I had to shift gears.

Felicity wasn't interested in what I wanted to say, only in keeping me off balance. "I have something to talk to *you* about," she said. "Come into my office."

She turned away and headed down the corridor. I stared after her. I had a head full of Irene Haskell and Ivy Samuels Tree. I had a nascent ulcer full of vanity presses. I had a three-foot walk to a Rolodex that undoubtably contained, among other things, the phone number of an ex-receptionist named Janet.

I tried to put it all out of my mind. Unless Janet was the kind of person who wrote her own address and number under "Me," I would have to know her last name before I could look her up. There was no point in thinking about vanity presses. That was an argument I couldn't win in this office. As to Irene Haskell and Ivy Samuels Tree—I couldn't ask Felicity questions about them unless I was talking to Felicity.

I hurried down the corridor until I got to her office. When I came in, she didn't rise, and she didn't suggest we go to the conversational grouping. She sat behind the mahogany desk, frowning at her telephone pad.

"I got a call this morning," she said, "from a Miss Amelia Samson."

She looked at me as if expecting explication. I didn't give it to her. Amelia Samson "writes" a romance book a week, all of which come out in her own line, called Amelia Samson's Love-lines, from Dortman and Hodges. She's got the world's definitive collection of Worth gowns. She appears on every major television network and in every national magazine at least twice a year. Johnny Carson makes jokes about Amelia on the *Tonight Show*. Felicity knew who Amelia Samson was.

"Miss Samson," Felicity said, "wanted to talk about pseud-onyms. She wants to write her article on the importance of pseudonyms—picking them, that is, and suiting them to the kind of romance book you write."

I shrugged. "She should know," I said. "She's very good at what she does."

"*Writing* magazine," Felicity said, "does not approve of pseud-onyms."

It took me a minute to take this in. My mind was still half on Ivy, and wandering around the problem of how to find Janet's last name. Then I realized Felicity was not opening a negotiation. She was making a categorical statement.

"What do you mean you don't approve of pseudonyms?" I said. "People use pseudonyms. Amelia Samson didn't start out being called Amelia Samson."

"I'm *aware* people use pseudonyms," Felicity Aldershot said. "I said *Writing* doesn't approve of them. We don't approve of them under any circumstances, but we especially don't approve of them when they're owned by the publishing company."

"Neither does the American Writers of Romance," I said. "At least, they don't approve of the names being company-owned rather than author-owned. They've been negotiating the point for the past five years. What are you going to do about it?"

"We're going to advise them to turn down any agreement that would require them to publish under a pseudonym exclusive to a particular house or line."

"Fine," I said. "Then they don't publish with any of the major lines, and they don't work for any of the major companies."

"*Writing* magazine has always stood up for the rights of writers," Felicity said.

"Crap," I said.

Felicity raised her eyebrows, but she wasn't disturbed. She had made her nonnegotiable demand. I would have to live with it.

I ignored it instead. "Do you remember Irene Haskell?" I said. I could have asked her if she were personally acquainted with the man in the moon. "The woman who wanted to sue you over Literary Services."

"Oh," Felicity said. "Yes."

"She was beaten up outside her apartment last night," I said. "Somebody tried to take her head apart with a baseball bat."

I was being as brutal as I could manage. It wasn't working. Felicity said, "How terrible," in a way designed to let me know she had only said it because it was expected of her. I sat on the other side of her desk and waited in vain for guilt to make her tremble.

"Didn't you say you were writing an article on line marketing?" she asked.

I was not defeated. I came out of Felicity's office still wearing my coat, my gloves, and all my scarves. If I hadn't been so busy trying to steal her expensive imitation Rolodex, I might have had time to get myself unwrapped. Instead, I had the Rolodex. It had a marble base. It weighed over five pounds. It was lying in the bottom of my shoulder bag, furnishing proof that the lady at Bloomingdale's had not been lying when she told me that bag was made of "the finest, softest, *strongest* leather in the world."

If I could get to my office and shut myself in, I could move the wardrobe and look through the Rolodex. I could answer two of my questions in one morning. If the Brookfields and Felicity left me alone.

The Brookfields had no intention of leaving me alone. Jack Brookfield was waiting for me outside the door to his office.

"Miss McKenna!" he said as soon as he saw me. "Miss McKenna! Please come in! We have something to show you!" He bounced up and down on the soles of his feet, making his soft body ripple under his clothes. "We're very excited about this," he babbled. "Very, very excited."

Through his open door I saw Stephen Brookfield and a rumpled collection of overworked peons meant to represent Staff. I hesitated. The weight of my shoulder bag was an insistent reminder of what I was *supposed* to do, what I had *promised* myself to do.

"We've spent all *morning* putting this together," Jack Brookfield said.

People who are eager to please are often just as eager to induce guilt. Jack Brookfield was no exception. He stood away from the door and made a flourishing gesture inviting me inside.

"We have coordinated our efforts on the romance project," he said.

"I've got work to do," I grudged. "I can't stay long."

Jack got me a chair. "We've worked out a schedule that will use all our divisions at once," he said. "We'll have a month of romance. We'll *celebrate* romance."

"Should have done it for Valentine's Day," I said. I slung my bag over the back of the chair he was holding for me—anything to keep it off my shoulder. Then I saw a pile of gloves and scarves on the heater near the window and walked over to it. I started to unwrap. There were many more gloves and scarves than people in the room. Jack, I decided, was the kind who was always forgetting his gloves in the office and having to stop for a new pair on the way home.

"Literary Services," Jack said, "is sponsoring a special romance novel—uh—sale." The word "sale" seemed to defeat him. "For the whole romance month," he said, "we'll evaluate any new romance manuscript at half our usual cost." He beamed.

Stephen Brookfield snorted. The Staff moaned.

"What are those?" I said.

I was pointing to the wall behind him. Jack turned to stare at the sixteen framed *Writing* magazine covers, as if he'd never noticed them before. I'd noticed them as soon as I walked into the office. The first two in the first row were in English. The rest were in an assortment of languages and alphabets. *Writing* magazine was apparently published in Chinese, Japanese, Greek, and Turkish as well as English, French, and German.

Jack Brookfield turned back to me. "Aren't you interested in romance month?" he asked.

"Maybe she wants you to talk sense," Stephen said. "Are you capable of talking sense?"

"What doesn't make sense?" Jack said. "I'm talking about a great opportunity, for ourselves and for our clients. Romance is a very big area of publishing."

"Getting smaller all the time," Stephen said.

"I don't know what you mean," Jack said.

"Look," I said, "in the first place, what do you know about romance novels?"

Stephen saw immediately what I was doing. He sat back in his chair and gave me his Richard Burton smile. Jack was completely mystified.

"We publish a romance line here," he said. "And we study the market. That's our job, you know. Studying the market."

"You publish a fourth-rate romance line here," I said. "You couldn't get the things you publish past an editorial assistant at Second Chance at Love or Silhouette. You're still using the bitchy, sophisticated Other Woman. You're five years out of date."

"I'm sure I wouldn't know," Jack said. He didn't tell me what he wouldn't know. The sentence had so little connection with anything that had been said, I assumed it was just an excuse for making noise.

I looked around the room at Stephen and the Staff, trying to decide how to go about saying what I wanted to say next. The Staff was bored. They were used to having an idiot for a boss, used to taking the consequences. Stephen Brookfield was expectant. He thought I was going to discourse at length on what I thought Jack Brookfield should have had as qualifications for his job.

I took a deep breath. "I could spend the rest of the day arguing with you about romance," I said, "except I haven't got the rest of the day and I don't have the stomach for it anyway. That Mrs. Haskell who was giving you so much trouble got beaten into a coma last night, I've spent twelve of the past twenty-four hours talking to police and lawyers, and I'm dead tired. All I want to do—"

"It's going off like Vesuvius," Stephen said.

Jack stared at him. I wanted reactions. I got them. The Staff looked distressed, the way any subway newspaper reader would look distressed by news of random violence. Jack and Stephen were beyond that. I wondered what I'd wanted from them, an expression of guilt? I didn't get it. They were staring at each other with a kind of fascinated horror. Jack looked on the verge of breaking down. Stephen was a step away from hysterical laughter.

I had a crazy desire to ask Jack about the paperweight on his desk the way I'd asked him about the *Writing* covers—anything to change the conversation, to get myself back into control of the situation. Then the situation got back into control of itself. Stephen relaxed in his chair. Jack straightened a few things on his desk, cleared his throat, turned his face to me, and started smiling again.

"Our romance newsletter," he said, "is doing a special edition. It'll have three times the usual pages for romance month. The romance newsletter is published in sixteen languages and sold in twenty-two countries."

"I find I have a need to excuse myself," Stephen said. He gave Jack a really nasty little smile. He wasn't Richard Burton this time. He was Vincent Price in *The Conqueror Worm*. "Nature calls."

I watched, fascinated, while they engaged in another staring match. There was nothing confusing about this one. Stephen wanted to leave. Jack didn't approve of his going, or what he was going for.

Stephen got out of his seat, shook out his pants creases, and bowed to me. Then he bowed to Jack and walked out the door.

"This is going to take teamwork," Jack called after him. "This is a very big project. We're all going to have to work together."

Stephen didn't answer. Maybe he hadn't heard. Jack turned his attention to me and worked up a big, hearty smile.

"A coordinated effort," he said, as if nothing had happened to change the subject since I first walked into his office.

I got out my cigarettes and settled in for a long haul.

THIRTY-ONE

It *was* a long haul—over an hour. Jack had projections, statistics, business philosophies, aesthetics, illustrations, and tangents. I had a head full of questions and resentments. *Something* had happened between Stephen and Jack. Something about the beating of Irene Haskell—or my knowledge of it—had frightened them both. I was in no position to know which of those possibilities scared them, or why.

If the Staff hadn't been in attendance, I might have tried to strong-arm Jack. It had worked once before. It might work again. The presence of peons-as-audience made that tactic unworkable. I knew Jack as an appeaser. I had no idea what he'd do to appease the six nondescript figures sitting in a semicircle behind me. Lie, probably, or ignore my questions. Unlike Hercule Poirot, I am not adept at spotting lies and using them against the liar.

I allowed myself to be subjected to a lecture on The Psychology of the Unpublished Writer. Jack seemed to have researched this subject at length.

"Their attitude to the business," he told me, "is that it's an unscalable wall, an unclimbable mountain, an impossibility. If you could get past what they say they think to what they really think, you'd find they think no one ever gets published at all."

This was too much, even for me.

"Where do they think books come from?" I asked him.

"Books are written by people who have always been writers and will always be writers," Jack said. "They—the unpublished writers—are people who have never been writers and will never be writers. World without beginning or end."

I was curious. "You try to talk them out of this?" I said.

Jack was appalled. "Oh, *no*. It's the state of mind we're looking for. The optimum Writing Enterprises client is someone who expects failure—who even wants failure."

There was a snicker from one of the Staff, telling him he'd gone too far. He blushed furiously.

"Not that we want them to fail," he said. "We're here to show them how wrong they are."

He scanned the group behind me. Their expressions must have been particularly disapproving. Jack started straightening his desk again. Since he had already straightened it four times, he was reduced to moving everything on it into a new position.

"Once they've succeeded," he said, "they're no longer our clients." He brightened. "Our job is to make ourselves obsolete."

Someone behind me whispered, "As long as there's one born every minute, we'll *never* be obsolete." Someone else giggled.

I grabbed the strap of my shoulder bag and started to get up. "Mr. Brookfield," I said.

"Jack," Jack said.

"This has all been very interesting, but I've been here more than an hour. If I intend to get any work done—"

"Work?" He said the word like a Maori tribesman would say "television."

"There isn't going to be a romance month without a special

romance section, and there isn't going to be a special romance section unless I get down to my office and work on it."

Jack said, "Oh." He thought I was giving him an excuse. He thought I was politely telling him I didn't like him. He was half-right.

I scooted for the door, unwilling to give him time to think of a new essential matter for discussion.

"You ought to write your philosophy down," I said as I disappeared into the corridor. "They could use it as an article in *Writing* magazine."

I don't know what made me feel worse—that I'd said it, or that Jack Brookfield looked pleased.

I did not head for my office. I did not plunge immediately into solving the problems of the wardrobe and Janet's last name. I started looking for Stephen Brookfield instead.

He wasn't in his office. He wasn't in the reception area, Felicity Aldershot's office, or the Art Department, either. I asked the art assistants still occupying the floor of the reception area if he'd gone out. They said no.

I returned to the central core of offices, wishing they'd said yes. If Stephen had not left and could not be found, there was only one place he could be. I stood in front of the door marked MEN and argued with myself. There might be five or six stalls beyond that door and a man in every one of them. There might be half a dozen open urinals, all in use. There might be a condom dispenser. I wasn't sure condom dispensers were legal in the state of New York.

I looked up and down the corridor. It was empty. I stood very still and listened for approaching footsteps. There were none. I opened the door and went inside.

If Alida Brookfield hadn't been cheap—or a female supremacist, as Martin Lahler called her—there might have been half a dozen urinals, five or six stalls, and a condom dispenser. Instead, there were two stalls, no urinals, and a sink. One of the stalls was empty. I could hear Stephen Brookfield's muffled laughter coming from the other.

There was a latch-lock on the door to the corridor, and I used it. Then I walked across the dirty white-tiled floor and knocked on the door of the stall Stephen had hidden himself in.

"Come *out* of there," I said. "I don't want to stay in here any longer than I have to."

The laughter stopped. Stephen said, "Jesus Christ."

"I have something of yours," I said. "I locked the outside door."

There was the sound of metal sliding against metal. Stephen slid the stall door open and peered out at me. His eyes were very dark and bright. His hands were limp.

"You're out of your mind," he said. "You're not supposed to be here."

I unzipped the safety compartment in my bag and took out the glassine envelope.

"It was in one of the books you gave me yesterday," I said. "I found it."

"You found it." He took it from me. He turned it over and over in his hand. Then he slipped it into the breast pocket of his suit jacket. He smiled as if he'd caught me out in a trick I was trying to play on him. "Why don't I think you're just being a good Samaritan?"

I backed up until I was leaning against the sink. Everything was slow motion for Stephen. His speech was slow, his movements were slow, even his thinking was slow. It was all very correct, but whatever he did or said took forever. It gave me time to think. What I thought about was how out of place I was in that room.

Stephen came all the way out of the stall. "If you're not being a good Samaritan," he said. "You must want something."

That was true enough. I tried to remember what it was I wanted. I had wanted to confront Stephen and was now confronting him. I had never actually defined what I wanted to confront him about.

I started with the obvious. "That costs a lot of money," I said. "You have to get the money from somewhere. I want to know where you get the money."

"You want to know where I get the money for *dope?*"

"Jack's stealing from petty cash," I said. "You told me so yourself. Michael was embezzling. What are you doing?"

"If I was doing something, why would I tell you?"

I thought that one over. "I don't know," I said.

Stephen sighed. I was no longer an object of suspicion. I was pitiful. He walked across to the radiator and leaned against it, crossing his arms over his chest.

"You said you played a half-assed role in the Agenworth case," he said. "Now I believe it. Do you really think, if I *was* selling the family silver, I'd tell you about it? Just because you asked?"

"I brought back the envelope," I said.

"There are plenty more envelopes," Stephen Brookfield said. "There are envelopes stretching from here to the end of created history." He shook his head sadly. "You don't even know the right questions," he said.

"I'll tell you what I do know," I said. "I know they ran a check on you, on all of you, after Michael was murdered. They went into all your finances. They didn't find anything on you. I know something else, too. I know that stuff costs a lot of money. As I said before. Where are you getting the money for it?"

"Maybe I'm not using that much of it."

"Look in the mirror. Make a videotape of one of your days in the office."

"Maybe it's not costing me any money."

He laughed at the look of shock on my face. He had shifted the atmosphere. He was no longer the potential friend of late in our talk in my office. He had returned to the Graham Greene novel. I could easily hate him when he was like that. He *did* ooze. He was sweaty and dirty and insinuating. "McKenna, McKenna, McKenna," he said. "Didn't they teach you Aristotle in that fancy college you undoubtedly went to? Didn't you ever read Ayn

Rand? Contradictions cannot and do not exist. Paradoxes, yes. Contradictions, no."

"Which is supposed to mean what?" I said.

"Which is supposed to mean that, when you have rid yourself of everything that is not an elephant—"

"Don't quote clichés to me," I said. "You're not making any sense."

"I have not been stealing any money, at least not in quantities big enough for anyone to find. That's true. I'll tell you something else that's true. I do use a lot of it. And something else. I get paid exactly fifteen thousand dollars a year, and I have never earned a bonus. All those things are true. Of course, I've had the clothing allowance and my rent, but you'll find Alida paid for those as bills were presented to her. I never saw any of that money."

"Which is supposed to mean you haven't been paying for the drugs," I said.

He shrugged again. "Don't ask me," he said. "You're the one who came running in here, bent on interrogating me."

"I wasn't *interrogating* you, goddamn it." I grabbed a cigarette from the pack in my pocket, lit it, and threw the match on the floor. There were a lot of matches on the floor. There were a lot of cigarette butts, too. I wondered if the cleaning lady had ever ventured in here.

"You don't pay for it and if I can figure out why you don't pay for it, then I can explain everything," I said. "That's what you're *saying.*"

"I'm not saying anything."

"You want me to figure it out," I said. "That's why you asked me if it were true I solved the Agenworth mess. You want somebody to figure it out. Why bother to wait till I figure it out? Why not just tell me?"

A smile, a shake, a shrug: sequence in slow motion. Graham Greene was gone. I wondered what was coming next, *The Sound of Music?*

What came next was a request for a cigarette. I lit one and gave it to him.

"All I want," Stephen Brookfield said, "is to be allowed to commit suicide in peace."

"What?"

"I could give you a lot of crap about my childhood," he said, "but I'm thirty-four, not thirteen, and no matter how crappy it was, I know it's no excuse. Let me try to make this perfectly clear. I take a lot of dope. I am perfectly aware that by taking a lot of dope I am killing myself. I don't give a shit."

"You must give a shit," I said. "If you really wanted to commit suicide, you'd just do it."

"What for?"

"What do you mean what for?" I said. "Because you wanted to."

"I don't have that violent a temperament," Stephen said. "I don't hate myself. I'm not facing financial or social ruin. I'm not morbidly depressed. I just don't care. Why should I jeopardize—any more than I have to—a situation that has almost nothing but advantages for me?"

"Because it has *almost* nothing but advantages?" I suggested.

"Very good," Stephen said.

He dropped his half-smoked cigarette to the floor and stepped on it. He was completely relaxed. It had to be heroin, I decided. Heroin relaxed you, and it lasted a relatively long time. All the reports I'd heard about cocaine said it speeded you up and was over very quickly.

I thought about that scene in Jack Brookfield's office. Stephen had needed calming down *then*.

"'It's going up like Vesuvius,'" I quoted. "What did you mean?"

"It was a description," Stephen said. "A very apt description."

"Talk *sense*," I said.

Stephen shook his head. "You ought to get out of here. Somebody's going to want to use the facilities soon and then . . ." His voice trailed off suggestively. He almost leered.

I wasn't ready to give up.

"If you want me to figure it out, you have to give me more," I said.

"I've given you everything you need," he said. "First, figure out who's giving it to me. Then," his smile was full and clear. "Then figure out *why*."

"God *damn* you," I said. I felt as if I'd been saying it all morning.

Stephen made a clucking sound. "I'll leave you with one more thing," he offered, "in case you do the obvious thing and start worrying about my motives. Like all suicides, I'm very possessive about my death. I don't intend to let God determine it. I don't intend to let anyone else determine it either." He grabbed my elbow. "The door," he said. "I'll be a gentleman and make sure the coast is clear."

THIRTY-TWO

The coast was so clear, I wondered if Stephen Brookfield had kept me in the men's room long enough for everybody else to abscond to Brazil. Marty Lahler's door was shut. The lights were out in the Art Department. I hurried down the hall to my office, not waiting to see if Stephen came out behind me or which way he went if he did. I slipped inside, turned on the overhead light, and shut the door. Then I pulled the desk to block the door, just in case. Peace and quiet, finally.

The wardrobe was heavier than I'd expected. Worse, what had been a bulky piece of furniture in the first place had been made more recalcitrant by the swelling and warping of the wood. Every time I pushed it it moved, but only slightly. It made a high, nerve-sanding whine.

After three of those whines, I sat down, lit a cigarette, and reconsidered the project. The inner walls were all pasteboard. The sound of the wardrobe against the linoleum had to be clear as far away as Felicity Aldershot's office. If I continued trying to move that monstrosity, somebody was going to come just to find out what the terrible noise was.

I put my cigarette in a tin ashtray on the floor, got up, and tried pushing it again. This time I managed to move it three quarters of an inch. I also managed to produce a sound like a buzz saw attacking steel. I stopped, held my breath, and waited. If no one came this time, there was no one to come. The first of my possible explanations for the wardrobe had to be the right one. There had to be something special about it in its original position. No one would rig it so that it had to be moved to be of use. If, of course, it had had any use besides serving as a place to store mops. If it hadn't, what had Michael Brookfield been doing in it?

I closed my eyes and counted ten. If no one came before the end of the count, I would move it another half inch.

There was a knock on the door.

"Miss McKenna?" Marty Lahler said. "Are you all right, Miss McKenna?"

Of all the people to show up now, it had to be Marty Lahler. After the Russian Tea Room fiasco, there would never be a good time for him to arrive, but there was something very fitting about his picking the worst possible moment. I moved the desk away from the door by picking it up and carrying it across the room. I didn't want it making its own sounds on the floor. I didn't want Marty to know I'd barred the door.

I tucked a pile of manilla envelopes under my arm (to give the impression I'd been working on the section) and let him in.

"You *are* all right," he said when he saw me. "I heard—I mean, I thought—you weren't screaming?"

"No," I said. "I wasn't screaming."

"Oh," he said. Then, "Your hands are all black."

I looked at my hands. There was a thick stripe of grime across one palm. The other was clean. I rubbed the dirty one against my pants.

"Is something wrong in the office?" he asked.

I made up my mind. Marty Lahler was too stupid to have committed the murders. He was too naive even to consider the possibility that someone he knew might have committed the murders.

"The wardrobe's out of place," I told him. "The police must have moved it. I was trying to put it back."

"The wardrobe?" Blink, blink. Think, think. I wanted to wring his oblivious little neck. The wardrobe took up half the room.

"It's made indentations," I said. "See?"

He came over to consider the indentations. The consideration took a long time. Finally he said,

"I could help you move it. Or you could wait till the Art Department got back from lunch. Maybe you should wait."

"I can't wait," I said. "It's driving me crazy."

"There are very big boys in the Art Department," Marty Lahler said. "Strong. They could pick something like this up."

He could only say that because he hadn't tried to pick it up himself. I'd have been surprised if Nick could move it without effort, and Nick is the biggest person I know. I did not, however, want to give Marty reasons to leave the manual labor to the "big boys" in the Art Department. I wanted that wardrobe *moved*.

"If we do it together," I said. "It won't be that hard."

He looked as if I'd told him I believed in the Tooth Fairy.

"I've already got it halfway there by myself," I said. "It's only a little farther. A couple of pushes."

He went to the far side of the wardrobe and stood there, awaiting execution.

"I suppose this is what you're like," he said. "I mean, when you want things done, you just get up and do them yourself."

"I take my clothes to the dry cleaner," I said. "Just like anyone else."

"Oh, so do I, so do I," Marty Lahler said. "That's not what I meant. You know what I meant."

"Place your hands here." I indicated a place on the wardrobe. "Brace your feet. On the count of three, push. Ready? One, two, three."

We moved it an inch and a half. We also moved it a little away from the wall. I went around to the front of it and kicked it back. It was far less difficult to move back to front than side to side.

"It would be a lot easier if they hadn't gone out to lunch," Marty said. "I mean, Miss Aldershot and Mr. Jack Brookfield went out to lunch, I saw them leave. Mr. Stephen Brookfield just disappeared. He does that sometimes. But with all of them gone, everybody else went too."

"What?"

"The staff. With nobody to watch over them, they went. Out. To lunch. I think some of them went to bars."

"Get in position again," I said.

Marty complied. "They leave me with all the papers," he said, "and half the time I can't figure them out. They're in all kinds of languages. What I say is, if they want to be international, they ought to hire some extra people who know languages. I don't know any languages."

"You know English," I said.

"That's right," Marty said.

I didn't give him time to work this out. "Get ready," I said. "One, two, *three.*"

We moved it another inch and a half. Marty beamed. He was more than just proud of himself. He was acquiring self-confidence. For Marty Lahler, self-confidence was a license to complain.

"It was bad enough when it was just the magazine," he said. "When I started out here the magazine just went to the United States and Canada. Then it went to England. That wasn't so bad. Then it went *everywhere.* It seemed like every week there was someplace else, and the someplace had a different language or a different alphabet and they all had different money." He looked at me wisely. "It's the money I have to be concerned about," he said.

"One more push," I said.

He nodded and got into position. "And then it wasn't just the magazine anymore," he said. "First it was Newsletters. Then it was Literary Services. Then it was Publishing. Now it's Writing Schools and Correspondence Courses."

"Felicity told me about it," I said. "One, two, *three.*"

This time we gave a long shove. I felt the wardrobe shudder, teeter, then settle into the indentations. I stepped back and looked at it. Marty looked at it, too. He looked as if he loved it so much, he would marry it.

"Well," he said. "That wasn't so hard."

He had red welts all over his hands, but I didn't mention them. I thought it would do him good to play macho.

"Now I can stop worrying about it," I said. "I hate it when things are out of place." In truth, I never know when things are out of place. I'm one of the world's untidiest, most disorganized people. Except about work, and I get paid for that.

Marty took my self-evaluation as gospel. "You're just like Miss Brookfield," he said. "She liked a place for everything and everything in its place." I wondered what Marty Lahler's childhood had been like. "The international stuff drove her crazy, too. She wanted to keep an eye on everything and she couldn't. When Mr. Michael Brookfield went to Europe he was supposed to stop in at our places and see how we were doing, and he always said he did, but she didn't believe him. She didn't trust him. She wanted to see for herself."

"Why didn't she?" I dropped into the chair and lit another cigarette. That Alida Brookfield had not trusted Michael was not news. If Marty couldn't give me news, I wanted him out of my office. In another time and place I might have been more charitable. In *that* time and place I wanted to climb into the wardrobe and look around.

"Miss Brookfield was afraid to fly," Marty said. "She didn't trust airplanes."

"Oh," I said.

"Miss Aldershot went once," Marty said. "She took a tour. But mostly it was Michael. And Michael always went with—um —a friend, you see."

"Yes," I said. "I see."

Marty Lahler clasped his hands behind his back, stared at his feet, and took a deep breath. I knew what was coming. I couldn't keep myself from wincing.

"You haven't had any lunch," Marty announced. "Would you like to have lunch with me?"

"Well," I said. What was I supposed to say? No? I prayed to the god of the Russian Tea Room and said, "I'm meeting a friend for lunch. I've got a few things to finish up here and then I'm leaving for the day."

"Oh," Marty Lahler said. The macho was gone. "You must have a lot of friends."

He meant, "You must have a lot of lovers." I almost told him to say so. Instead, I took him by the arm, pressed vigorous thanks in his ear, and led him to the door.

"I'll be here another week and a half," I said. "Maybe you'll give me a raincheck."

"We could go tomorrow," Marty said.

"I don't know about tomorrow," I said. "I don't know if I'll be in."

"I can't Thursday," Marty said. "Thursday I have a financial meeting. We all have lunch in Miss—Miss Aldershot's—office Thursdays."

"We'll talk about Friday when it gets here," I said, getting him into the hall. Then I thanked him again, shut the door in his face, and headed across the room to the wardrobe. As I crossed the floor, I said a grace prayer so perfect, God was going to expect me to sit down at a seven-course banquet for twenty and finish it myself. I got all the way to the end of it before I realized I'd forgotten something.

I opened the door, stuck my head into the hall, and yelled, "Marty!" at the top of my lungs. He came running. The look on his face increased my guilt the way helium increases the size of a balloon. If I had to look at him much longer, I was going to explode into expiation.

There was no point in being polite. "You remember Janet?" I asked him. "The receptionist?"

He nodded, very slowly. This was not what he expected. He didn't know how to maneuver the conversation around to what he expected.

"Do you remember her last name?" I asked him.

He said, "Miss Grasky," and waited. He wanted an explanation. I had none to give him.

"I hate thinking of her as just 'Janet,'" I said. "It's so impolite."

This was no explanation at all. He was going to ask questions.

I wasn't going to wait for them. I gave him another "goodbye" and another "thank you" and another door in his face.

I fit easily into the wardrobe, even with the door closed. Most people would. Jack might have some difficulty because of his girth, but anyone else at Writing Enterprises could lock themselves in that portable closet and camp out for a week. I should say hide out. The point of locking yourself in a closet has to be not to be seen.

I put my finger through what I thought of as the peephole and hit something hard and smooth. Glass? I leaned over to look, bumping open the wardrobe door. I had a clear view into Marty Lahler's office, a much clearer view than I should have had. The hole in the pasteboard wall that lined up with the peephole had been plugged with glass, all right. Magnifying glass. The piece in the hole must have come from something larger. The view was jagged and distorted at the edges. In one small area near the top, there was no visibility at all. Where I could see, however, I had better than perfect vision.

It was *what* I could see that bothered me. I'd expected Marty's desk. I got the right side of Marty's assistant's desk. A sheet of paper was taped to the gray metal desk top. Typed at the top was

DISTRIBUTION BY DIVISION—*February.* Underneath were lists. The *Writing* magazine list went:

Australia	56,462
Belgium	44,224
France	57,982
Germany	77,648
Great Britain	78,264
Greece	92,267
Ireland	45,231
Italy	96,341
The Netherlands	22,481
Sweden	31,672
Switzerland	21,484

I backed out of the wardrobe. Distribution figures? Why would anyone want to know how many copies of *Writing* magazine had been shipped to Switzerland in February? And why go to all this trouble to read Marty's assistant's list? Distribution figures are not like financial information. No one goes out of his or her way to make a secret of them, unless they're phenomenally bad. Writing Enterprises thought *their* distribution figures were wonderful. Writing Enterprises included their distribution figures in their press releases. Writing Enterprises kept a running count on the circulation of *Writing* magazine on a chalkboard in the lobby. Cramming yourself into that wardrobe and squinting through the peephole wouldn't get you one piece of information you couldn't get more easily somewhere else. Especially if you were Michael Brookfield.

I sat down, lit a cigarette, and tried to make it make sense. I couldn't. I told myself Michael Brookfield was a stupid man who'd made a stupid mistake. I couldn't believe that either. Then I came up with a brilliant idea. Marty's assistant had to have those distribution figures long before anyone else. She'd get them, type them up, and send them around as memos. She might even be the one who put the figures on the chalkboard. If someone wanted those figures *before* anyone else saw them, or maybe just earlier than they'd be released, the peephole would make sense.

That is, it *would* have made sense if I'd had the answer to a very simple question.

Whatever *for?*

In the office next door, Marty started humming "As Time Goes By." He was very, very off key.

I got the marble-based imitation Rolodex from my bag. If I couldn't make sense out of the wardrobe, maybe I'd do better with Janet Grasky.

Janet Grasky's name was not filed under Grasky. It was filed under Janet.

THIRTY-THREE

Janet Grasky lived in Brooklyn. I spent a futile minute wondering if she lived near Irene Haskell and, if she did, what that would mean to the case. It would mean nothing. Everyone in New York lives near everyone else in New York, more or less. There isn't anywhere you can't get to by taxi, bus, or subway.

I spent another futile minute searching my office for my coat, gloves, and scarf. Then I remembered I hadn't had them when I left Jack Brookfield's office. I visualized the pile of scarves and gloves on Jack's radiator and nearly kicked myself in the ankle. I was tired of wasting time. If I got within five feet of Jack, I'd lose another half hour. Charts, statistics, graphs, projections, or the Philosophy of the Unpublished Writer, Jack would think of something.

Outside, it was below freezing and windy. I had no choice. I did my best to develop a hostile mien (on the theory I could scare him off) and marched down to Jack's office.

When I got there, I was brought up short. Jack's door was closed. A strange man's voice was coming through the thin wood.

"Five years," the man said. "For God's sake, Jack, five years."

Jack mumbled something I couldn't hear.

Whatever it was made the stranger very angry. "I know the issue's late," he said. "I know it's only come in today. I'm not talking about today, damn it. I'm talking about five years."

Mumble, mumble, from Jack. Snort, from the stranger.

"You know what I'm carrying on you? Over half a million dollars. Christ, Jack, it isn't even legal. I'm your friend, I'm your friend—I'm as much your friend as anyone could be—but I can't carry half a million dollars. I can hardly carry it when you're paying up on time, there are *laws* about margin, Jack, and you're breaking every one of them, but when you're paying up I can cover it. I can make it look all right. Right now it stinks and my boss is beginning to smell it. If you can't come up with something, I'm going to have to shut you down."

"The issue just came in today," Jack Brookfield squeaked. "I can get it for you by Friday."

"Shit," the man said. "By Friday we'll all be on our way to Leavenworth."

I recognize a filibuster dead end when I hear one. Jack and his angry friend had come to that point in their argument when all they could, or wanted, to do was repeat the positions they'd established in louder and louder voices. I could eavesdrop all day without learning any more than I already knew.

I rapped loudly on the door. Inside, the voices stopped. There was a sound of furniture sliding against carpet.

"Yes?" Jack Brookfield said.

"It's Pay McKenna," I said. "I left my coat in your office."

More furniture moving. Jack Brookfield opened the door and peered out at me, squinting.

"Miss McKenna?"

"I left my coat in your office," I repeated. "When I was her this morning. Also my gloves and about six scarves. I don't mean to interrupt you, but if I could come in and get them?"

"Oh," Jack Brookfield said. Then, "Of course, of course. You're not interrupting anything. Mr. Dunne and I were just finishing."

He stepped back to let me inside. The stranger, a Wall Street type in a gray pin-striped three-piece and a white shirt with a starched collar, stood when he saw me.

"This is Miss Patience Campbell McKenna," Jack said. "She's here to work on the romance section."

Mr. Dunne had never heard of the romance section. He nodded politely.

"This is Thomas Dunne," Jack Brookfield said.

"Waycroft, Hammer and Dunne," Mr. Dunne said. He took out a small leather case, extracted a card, and handed it to me. He was a young man, in his early thirties. I decided he must be the son, if not the grandson, of the Dunne in the title. Waycroft, Hammer and Dunne was one of the older, and theoretically more conservative, brokerage firms. Nobody made partner over there until he or she was at least forty-five.

Mr. Dunne's card had WAYCROFT, HAMMER AND DUNNE: SECU-RITIES BROKERS engraved at the center. Mr. Dunne had written his name and extension number in green ink in the lower right-hand corner.

"Are you in the market?" he asked me. This was half polite-ness and half an assessment of the cost of my sweater. Mr. Dunne had a very good eye for sweaters.

"I'm in coats," I told him gravely. "If you gentlemen will just excuse me, I'll get mine from this pile and rush off."

"No hurry," Jack Brookfield said. "No hurry at all."

"I'm in a hurry," I said. I was, too. It didn't take Mr. Dunne's ant scowl to convince me I wanted out of that office fast. I my coat from the pile on the radiator and sorted hur-ugh scarves, then through gloves. The glove situation mpossible. My gloves were black. So were Jack Brookfield's—all fifteen pairs of them. I settled on some that looked likely and stuffed them into the pockets of my coat.

"Well," I said. "I'll just be going."

"No hurry," Jack said.

"Nice to have met you," I said to Mr. Dunne.

"Emma Willard," Mr. Dunne said.

"Right," I said.

"Vassar?"

"Greyson."

"Dear Lord," Mr. Dunne said. "Keep the card."

"I will," I said. Then I escaped into the hall.

It wasn't much of an escape. I turned the corner into the first corridor just as Felicity Aldershot reached her office door and dropped my bag just as she stopped fiddling with her keys. She looked up, saw me, and waved.

"I'm glad you're here," she said. "I was going to come looking for you."

She was doing sweetness and light, and doing it very well. It made me suspicious.

"I wanted to be sure you knew about the party tonight," she said. She walked toward me, smiling broadly. She reached me at almost the same moment Mr. Dunne decided to raise his voice again.

"Five years, Jack," Thomas Dunne shouted. "This has been going on for five whole *years.*"

"I *know* how long it's been going on," Jack shouted back.

Felicity frowned in the direction of Jack's office. Then she shrugged, turned away, and took my arm.

"It's a belated Saint Valentine's Day," she said, leading me away like an expert prison guard escorting an addled prisoner to her cell. "We had it all planned for the fourteenth, but everything was so up in the air on the fourteenth. So we're going to have it tonight."

"Tonight?"

I had a hard time imagining the scene of two murders as a

setting for a party. It gave Felicity Aldershot no trouble at all. She stopped at the door to her office. I looked inside and thought I was hallucinating. The place was crammed with boxes, huge rectangular boxes piled one on top of the other and squeezed side by side. The conversational grouping had been pushed into a corner. The bar had been folded into the wall. There was hardly room to move.

"Spot check," Felicity laughed. "Every month we go through at least one box from each of the countries we sell *Writing* magazine. Just to make sure everything's all right, you see. You could find *Writing* in any one of seventeen languages in this room."

"There have to be more than seventeen boxes," I said.

"Of course there are. But every country doesn't have its own language."

The box just inside the door was stamped with Greek letters I couldn't read. "I have a friend who speaks Greek," I told Felicity Aldershot. "He might get a kick out of one of those."

I wondered if I were imagining the sudden stiffness in Felicity's body, the swift hostility in her eyes. It came and went before I had adequate time to think about it. When she spoke again she was deliberately, mockingly gracious.

"Let me get you a Greek one from the closet," she said. "We ship some of those to Astoria and the Greek section of Chicago, you know. There's a substantial Greek-speaking population in the United States."

She hurried away to her closet, moving as quickly as the boxes would allow. As soon as she disappeared, I took a Greek edition from the box at my side and stuffed it in my bag. It was pure shoplifting, an activity I didn't approve of and had never before engaged in. I could neither explain it nor correct it. Once I'd got it out of the box and into my bag, there wasn't enough time to get it out of my bag and back into the box without Felicity seeing me. What had I been thinking of? Spiting her? Or had I been reverting to a childish need not to do as I was told?

Felicity came back with another Greek edition in her hand and handed it to me.

"Try not to forget the party," she said. "From four to six in reception. We'd like to get a picture of you for our staff section."

I had an overwhelming desire to get out of Felicity's office and never come back. Felicity was still being sweetness and light. The guiltier I felt, the more genuine she seemed.

I said, "Yes, yes, of course," and started edging toward the door, holding the second Greek edition in my hand.

"Our readers feel so much more *included* when they see a picture," Felicity said.

I said something like, "Of course they do," and made it into the corridor.

She finally realized something was wrong. She frowned at me the way she'd frowned in the direction of Jack's door.

"Are you all right?" she asked me. "You look a little under the weather."

"I'm fine," I said. "I'm meeting a friend for lunch."

"What's wrong with your hands?" she asked. "They're all black."

I shoved my hands into my pockets.

"I'm fine," I repeated. "I'm going to be late."

Then I made a break for the elevators.

THIRTY-FOUR

I thought about it all the way out to Brooklyn in the cab. I am a conventionally honest person. I do not think about morality. I do not think about what keeps me moral. I assume I am honest. I assume dishonest people are odd, or sick, or evil. Catching myself in an act of theft, however small, was unnerving. Catching myself stealing for no good reason at all was making me a little punch-drunk.

I didn't notice the weather (threatening snow) or the cab driver (threatening violence for being hauled out to Brooklyn). I kept going around and around that first Greek edition of *Writing* magazine. Prick a WASP and you get not just an ascetic, but an ethical nitpicker. I nitpicked all the way out to Park Slope. A couple of times I reached into my bag for the edition. I always stopped myself. I didn't want to touch the thing.

The cab driver pulled to a stop in the middle of a block of well-tended, elegant brownstones.

"Nice neighborhood," he said. "You gonna sit there all day or you gonna get out?"

"I'm getting out." I dug into my pockets, found a five and two ones, and gave them to him. He gave one of the ones back.

"That's a two-dollar tip," he said. "You don't want to give me a two-dollar tip. I wasn't that nice to you."

He was right. I took the dollar back, stuffed it into my coat, and ran to the sidewalk. The wind was even worse in Brooklyn than it had been in Manhattan. It got under my hair, making my ears stiff. Janet Grasky lived at 197 Park Street, Apartment 4D. The driver had stopped right in front of it. I started climbing the long, pretentiously majestic steps to the front door.

The buzzers were on the mailboxes in the vestibule. I pressed the one for 4D (Grasky/Heindon) and got an answering buzz in return. There was no intercom. As far as Janet knew, I could be a mugger. As far as I knew, the buzzer-answerer was Heindon (whoever that was). I started up the stairs—no elevator, of course, elegant brownstones never have elevators—and berated myself for not calling first. What was I going to tell Heindon if I saw her? Or, God forbid, him?

I needn't have worried. Janet was waiting for me at the top of the stairs, dressed in a long flannel nightgown and a battered flannel housecoat that came to her knees.

"You," she said when she saw me. "What are you doing here?"

It was a legitimate question. "There was something I wanted to ask you," I said, panting from the climb.

"You came all the way from Manhattan because there was something you wanted to ask me? Why didn't you phone?"

"I was in the neighborhood." It was the only lie I could think of. I hadn't phoned because it hadn't occurred to me. It should have occurred to me.

"Come in out of the hall," Janet said. "Mrs. Danowitz's probably got her eye to the door. Mrs. Danowitz *always* has her eye to the door."

I decided she meant the *crack* in the door. I followed her into a narrow entranceway, then through into a large, rambling living room. Apartments are bigger in Brooklyn than they are in Manhattan. They also tend to get more light. Janet's living room had four windows overlooking the street. Through them I could see the start of a new snowfall.

"If they want me to come back," Janet said, "you can tell them they can shove it. I mean, I've *had* it. Truly."

I took a seat on a chair that was two orange crates with cushions nailed to the bottoms and an Indian bedspread to cover.

"As far as I know, they don't want you back," I said, "but I wouldn't know if they did want you back."

"They wouldn't know if they wanted me back," Janet said. "They don't know what they want from one day to the other. You want coffee?"

"Coffee," I said. "Um—"

"I've got herb tea," Janet said, "but it's Susan's. Susan is such a cheap—never mind. Roommates. Know what my ambition in life is? To make enough money so I don't have to have roommates."

"You could get married," I said.

"Forget it," Janet said. "Another roommate. If you go by my brothers, a roommate who won't pick up after himself. You sure you don't want coffee?"

"No," I said. "That's all right. I wanted to ask you about

something, about—do you remember the day Michael Brookfield was murdered?"

She looked at me as if I were some kind of lunatic. "You're kidding," she said. "I mean, you have to be kidding. Why wouldn't I remember it? It made me a celebrity, for God's sake. First time I've ever gotten any recognition in this neighborhood. I took it down to the Marvellette and got a CPA with it."

"The Marvellette?"

"Singles bar. I'm always going to singles bars. They don't work but they may be worth it. My mother wants me to join the Sodality at church but that won't be worth it."

"I thought you didn't want to get married."

"I don't," Janet said.

I said, "Oh," and looked around for an ashtray. I found one. It was filled with Marlboro butts and the plastic ends of Tiparillos, but it would suit. It also answered a very important question. There was no unposted No Smoking sign in this apartment.

I lit a cigarette and threw the match in the tray, being careful the flame was out before the spent match struck plastic.

"It was what happened before Michael Brookfield's murder I wanted to ask you about," I said. "Or maybe after, but first before. You remember taking Ivy Samuels Tree in about quarter to four?"

"Taking her in?"

"To Michael Brookfield's office."

Janet gave the matter grave and deliberate thought. "She's the one in the newspapers," she said finally. "The black woman. The one looks like she belongs on the cover of Vogue." She looked at me. "*You* look like you belong on the cover of Vogue," she said. "Except maybe for the face."

"Right," I said. "Do you remember taking her in to see Michael Brookfield?"

"Nope," Janet said. "I buzzed Miss Brookfield for you, that I remember. Then that Felicity Aldershot person—God, she's a bitch, she was a bitch even before they made her head of the whole thing—anyway, Sweet Felicity wanted typewriter ribbons.

Can you believe it? A whole office full of typewriter ribbons, they're not good enough for her. The office typewriter ribbons are *silk*. She wants *nylon*. Nylon doesn't *smudge*." Janet shrugged. "She tells me to go out, I go out. I was gone about an hour."

"Right," I said. I was sitting upright, very alert and eager. She was giving me all the answers I wanted. "If you weren't the one who showed her in, then it must have been Felicity Aldershot—"

"Could have been Miss Brookfield," Janet said.

"No, it couldn't," I said. "I was with Alida Brookfield. It had to be Felicity Aldershot. Which means she had to be the one who told the police Ivy was there. Which means—" I stopped. I don't know what I thought I'd been doing, but it had just come apart in my hand. I took a deep breath and decided I needed more than another cigarette. I needed a drink.

"I thought you were going to tell me what it meant," Janet said.

I sighed. "It just occurred to me it didn't mean anything," I said. "For some reason or the other I had this idea it was the key. That whoever took Ivy in and told the police and then didn't tell anyone else in the office—no one knew about it, and you know what that place is like—"

"A sieve," Janet said virtuously.

"It just felt funny," I said. "That no one said anything, I mean. But it doesn't mean anything."

"Let me get you that coffee," Janet said. "You look like you need *something*."

"Just one more thing," I said, stopping her as she was about to walk out to the kitchen. "Did you type letters?"

"At Writing Enterprises? Yeah, sometimes."

"Did you type the letter Michael Brookfield sent to Ivy Samuels Tree?"

"No," Janet said. "But don't get your hopes up. They typed their own letters a lot. And Sweet Felicity Aldershot typed some when she had time. She was always doing other people's work for them. She was always letting us know what a saint it made her, too. I mean, I don't mind help when I need it, but I at least like to ask for it. I mean, she'd come up and tell you she'd done something for you you hadn't even asked her to do, and then she'd want you to be grateful for it. Have that coffee now. You look miserable."

"I am miserable," I said. As she headed for the kitchen, I had another thought, for once one mostly unconnected with the Brookfield murders. "Janet? What are you going to do now that you're not working at Writing Enterprises?"

Janet shrugged. "Look for a job. At least I will in a little while. I need a couple of weeks to calm down."

"I've got a friend named Joan Liddell. She runs a publishing business, a small one. They do romantic suspense. She's probably looking for people who can type."

"Yeah?" Janet was interested. "I'd like to get into a typing pool. You can go someplace from a typing pool. Everybody thinks receptionists are dumb."

"I've got her card in here somewhere," I said. The second Greek edition was folded in half and sticking out over the top of my bag. I threw it on the floor. Then I started rummaging in the debris, looking for my card case. I started taking handfuls of things and throwing them on the floor. The first Greek edition, the one I'd picked up from the box, came out with a pile of bills I hadn't got around to paying.

"You've got loose money in here," Janet said. "You shouldn't keep loose money in a bag without a top. You'll lose it."

"What loose money?" I looked up from my search. Like most forays into my bag, it was proving fruitless.

Janet held two one dollar bills in the air. "They fell out of this magazine," she said, holding the unfolded first Greek edition in the air. "I mean, I know we're all in a hurry sometimes, but money's *money.*" She shook the magazine for emphasis.

Dollar bills fell out of it like confetti from a party popper.

"It's the repeat performances," I told Janet, trying to stop laughing. I had been laughing for a long time. "You can never do anything once at Writing Enterprises. Two typewriter ribbon murders. Two stuffed publications."

"Two stuffed publications?" Janet was picking up the money and stacking it in piles of ten. She should have been in business school. She had such an exaggerated respect for the sheer physical fact of money.

"I took a romance book home from there," I said, "and it had a little envelope of dope in it. By accident."

"There's eight hundred dollars here so far," Janet said. "You can't tell me somebody put eight hundred dollars in that magazine by accident."

"No," I said. I could feel myself quietening. "This time it wasn't an accident, and it wasn't negligence, and it wasn't stupidity. She put them there because they belonged there."

"Nine hundred," Janet said. "It's going to be an even thousand. Somebody put a thousand dollars in a magazine and gave it to you on purpose?"

"Oh no," I said. "She didn't give it to me. In fact, she did her best to keep it away from me. I stole it."

"You stole it."

"I didn't know it was going to have a lot of money in it," I said. "I thought it was just a magazine. She was annoying me, so I took a magazine from a box she told me not to take a magazine from. They're all in on it," I said. "It's the only way it makes sense."

"The only way what makes sense?" Janet tapped the last stack. "One thousand."

I had been lying on my back on the floor, smoking and staring at the ceiling. Now I sat up and looked around for my coat. "Think about the piracy," Nick had said, telling me why he thought holding a writer's conference in Greece was a bad idea. "We always underestimate," Marty Lahler had said, talking about supplying genre books to Europe. And that peephole. No one was interested in Marty's financial figures. There was nothing wrong with them. I was sure every penny was accounted for, every fraction of a percent of tax paid. I knew why Michael

Brookfield wanted the distribution figures as fast as he could get them. I knew why Stephen Brookfield got his little glassine envelopes without paying for them. I even knew why Michael and Alida had to die and why Irene Haskell had to be got out of the way. The only thing I didn't know was who had done the killing.

I didn't know how I was going to prove any of it, either. I decided it wasn't my problem. I would dump the whole mess in Lu Martinez's lap and let him take care of it.

I spotted my coat thrown over the back of the orange crate chair. I got up, put it on, and shoved my hands in my pockets.

"I will explain all this," I told Janet. "I promise. As soon as I've talked to the police."

"I'll get you a bag for the money," Janet said. "It won't be as easy to carry in stacks like that."

I brushed the hair out of my face and started searching for a cigarette.

"What's that you've got all over your hands?" she asked me. "They're *black*."

THIRTY-FIVE

I called Ivy before I called Martinez. Actually, I called Nick to ask about Ivy. She was still the key, even if she didn't have evidence that would save her or prove someone else guilty. She *had* been set up, not once but three times. The first time, someone had gone to a lot of trouble over a considerable period to ensure her presence in the right place at the criminally necessary moment. If I could prove *that*, Ivy would have nothing to worry about. I couldn't prove it. The best anyone could do was prove which typewriter had been used to type Michael Brookfield's letter to Ivy. I had a feeling the answer would be uninteresting.

"Get hold of it and keep it anyway," I told Nick. "Just in case."

He was not optimistic. "If it came from Michael Brookfield's typewriter," he said, "it could do us more harm than good."

"I know," I said.

"She's in the hospital now," Nick said. "It's not as bad as before. She answers to her name and she eats and you can make conversation with her. Sort of."

"What's 'sort of'?" I asked.

"She'll talk about her children," Nick said. "She'll talk about the newspapers and what she sees on television and how she likes the hospital. If you try to ask her about what happened, she tells you she must have been sleepwalking."

"Dear Jesus," I said.

"I know," Nick said. "It's a crazy situation. The DA's office has lost all interest in the case. There's too much shrink evidence. They're never going to convict her and they know it. They may get her put away in a hospital for the criminally insane."

"That's worse," I said.

"That's worse," Nick agreed. "We may have an out on violence. She's showing no evidence of violence. Why should she? She was never violent to begin with."

"They won't believe that."

"The DA's office won't, no. Oddly enough, I think the police might."

"You think the police think she didn't do it?"

"I don't know," Nick said. "I'm not being very coherent. *Nothing's* being very coherent. I try to work on the case and there's nothing to work on. I don't have a client in any way that matters. I can't decide on the best approach. Hell, what's the best approach? No matter what I do, the only end I see is them putting her away. And I don't think she's snapped for good. Neither do the doctors."

"What do the doctors think?"

"Extended shock."

"Meaning they don't know."

"They can describe it," Nick said, "but they can't explain it. They can't cure it, either."

"That's bad," I said.

I had said nothing in particular and he responded by saying nothing in particular back. We went on like that for a while. There was nothing more to say. I could have explained things to him. He didn't want to hear it. He could have given me the technical details of Ivy's possible defenses. He knew I wouldn't understand them. I was making the call from a booth on lower Madison Avenue. The wind was going right through me. Neither of us seemed capable of getting off the phone.

Finally, Nick said something about having to meet Phoebe, and I said something about having another call to make. We listened to each other's silence.

"Maybe I'll come over tonight," Nick said. It was a concession. He'd been coming over much more often than he liked in the past month.

"Maybe I'll make curried chicken," I said. That was a concession, too.

Martinez agreed to meet me at the Park Luncheonette in half an hour. He gave me none of the trouble I'd anticipated. Expecting a good quarter hour on the phone marshaling arguments and storming barriers, I'd walked from Madison Avenue to the Writing Enterprises building, thrown the alcoholic concessionaire out of his phone booth, and settled into the warm. I was out again in less than a minute. Martinez not only agreed to talk to me, he admitted he was eager to talk to me. He'd been wanting to talk to me for days.

He'd talked to me the night before. I didn't make an issue of it. I got off the phone and considered the fact that I spent a lot of my time with Martinez not making an issue of things. Having a homicide detective for a friend is like having a very famous person as a neighbor. You efface yourself. You accept their version of reality as axiomatic. You never push.

You're always a little embarrassed to be seen with them in public.

I returned the phone booth to the concessionaire and walked down to the Park Luncheonette. It was deserted. I slid into a booth. I decided that, under the circumstances, meeting Martinez in a Greek coffee shop was very appropriate.

The waitress came up to take my order for hot chocolate.

"What's the matter with your hands?" she asked me. "They're all black."

There were smudges on both my palms. I looked at them and tried to think. There had been a smudge on one palm when I finished moving the wardrobe. Both my hands had been dirty at Janet's. I had washed them clean at Janet's.

Back up, I thought. There had been a smudge on my palm when I finished moving the wardrobe. There had been smudges on *both* my palms when I finished talking to Felicity Aldershot. There had been smudges on both my palms when I was at Janet's. Then I had washed my hands. Until I washed my hands, I could blame the smudges on the wardrobe. Where were they coming from now?

"It's not the end of the world," the waitress said. "I'll get you a Handi-Wipe." She hurried off, reminding me of Nick's mother. All the waitresses at the Park Luncheonette remind me of Nick's mother.

I reached into my pockets, pulled out my gloves, and laid them on the table. They were my gloves. I hadn't picked up a pair of Jack's by mistake. Jack couldn't have crammed his short, pudgy fingers into my cashmere-lined Saks Fifth Avenue specials.

The waitress came back with the Handi-Wipe. I took it out of its plastic-coated foil wrapper and cleaned myself off. Then I picked up the gloves again. When I looked at my fingers, they were smudged with black.

"You've developed a new method of fingerprinting," Martinez said, sliding into the other booth bench. "Do it yourself."

"Pick up the gloves," I told him. He gave me an odd look. I hadn't even said hello. I probably looked very white. He picked up the gloves and dropped them again.

"Look at your hands," I said.

"What'd you get on them?" Martinez said. He rubbed his black-smeared fingers together, as if that would clear them. "They must be filthy."

"Something we didn't think of," I said. "Somebody strangled two people with typewriter ribbons. Typewriter ribbons are inky. Why didn't anyone have ink on their hands?"

"I thought of gloves," Martinez said. "I didn't find any gloves." He tapped mine. "These are the gloves that were used in the murders?"

"Of course not," I said. "Those are my gloves. They were fine this morning."

Martinez took a deep breath. He was holding on to his temper. He may even have been holding on to his sanity.

"Let's start again," he said. "Hello, McKenna. I take it you're speaking to me again."

"You were the one who wasn't speaking to me," I said.

"It was mutual. Let's not argue about it." He pointed to the gloves. "That what you wanted to talk to me about?"

"Oh," I said. It started coming back to me. Janet. The money. I reached into my bag and came up with the plastic one. I pushed it across the table to Martinez. "That's what I called you about," I said. "Look inside it."

He looked inside it. "Jesus Christ," he said. "How much have you got in here? Where did you get it?"

"I got it out of this." I gave him the first (box) Greek edition. "It was in there, laid out between the pages. Page by page. I think. I mean, most of it fell out before I looked."

"Patience," Martinez said, being very patient. "You are not making any sense."

"I'm making perfect sense," I said. "Michael Brookfield was cooking his books. Jack Brookfield was stealing from petty cash. All of that's fine, you see, except it doesn't explain anything. It doesn't explain enough. Like the fact that Stephen Brookfield's financially clean—he just about told me we could look forever and not catch him stealing anything—but he's a heroin addict and he takes a lot of it and he doesn't have to pay for it. Explain *that*. And Jack Brookfield is into a brokerage house for half a million dollars and he couldn't even get margin for that out of petty cash."

"Jack's into some brokerage house for half a million dollars?"

"Waycroft, Hammer and Dunne," I said. "They're a very respectable house. And I figured out the wardrobe." I told him about the wardrobe. "So you see," I said, "it doesn't make sense except one way and that explains everything. Especially if you start with the money in the magazine, because the magazine was going to Greece, and all that money was going with it."

The waitress came up. Martinez asked for coffee and a bran muffin. The waitress beamed at us. Like Nick's mother, she enjoyed seeing young love in flower.

"Go very slowly," Martinez said. "From the beginning."

"All right," I said. "Start with two facts. First, Stephen Brookfield is a dope addict without the usual financial difficulties of dope addicts, a situation that cannot be explained by either his salary or an assumption of theft. He isn't stealing anything. If you check around, you'll find he's been telling me the truth."

"We *have* checked around."

"Next, there's a lot of loose cash floating around Writing Enterprises. Put one and one together and make two."

Martinez has always been good at this kind of thing. "Two," he said. "Someone's supplying."

"They all are, I think. They must be. It's too complicated an operation for one person."

"But we checked," Martinez said. "When Michael Brookfield died."

"You checked Michael Brookfield," I said. "Did you check, oh, Felicity Aldershot?"

"No," Martinez said. He flushed. *"No."*

"Maybe you should," I said. "Later. Right now, tell me something. Say they're low- to middle-level drug suppliers. What's the easiest way to catch them?"

"The *easiest* way?" Martinez said. "If you're not particular about what they're convicted of—and I'm surely not—then the easiest way is to hope the tax boys get them. That's the only truly wonderful thing about the Internal Revenue Service. They can put people away we couldn't touch otherwise."

"Add two and two," I said. "That money was going to Greece, in cash. The magazine has a big circulation in Greece. It isn't doing too badly in Italy, either. Except Nick was telling me something about Greece the other day. Non-Greek publishers do lousy in Greece. The Greeks don't read much and what they do read they read in their own magazines and newspapers and if they want something foreign some domestic company just pirates it." I tapped the table. "If you check, you'll probably find the same thing about Italy. And Spain. And some of the Latin American countries."

"Some of the magazines go to Italy?"

"The magazines go all over the place," I said. "Big boxes of them. Say there are forty magazines to a box, that's about standard in the business. One thousand per magazine, forty thousand per box. At least to Italy and Greece, Lu. Maybe to other places as well. Like I said, there were a lot of boxes."

Two and two was harder than one and one. "I know what you're saying," he said. "They're laundering it. It's going out as United States currency and it's being returned as foreign earnings on the sale of magazines—"

"Probably also literary service fees and paperback book sales," I said. "And they're holding a Writer's Conference on Kos this summer. Some of it will probably come back from there."

"But how will it come back? You can't just walk up to some bank in Athens and deposit forty thousand American dollars."

"You don't," I said. "There's a huge black market money system in Greece and Italy and places where the local money is highly inflationary. The black market gives better rates than the banks do. You get your money changed there—not too much of it, not in too-large bills, not with the same people over and over again, if you want to be careful—then you bring the drachmas to the bank and get them changed back. You probably make money on the deal."

"It's still a lot of floating cash," Martinez said.

"I know it is. They probably don't send a shipment every month. They couldn't, not if I'm right about how they're distributing it when it's here. And every time they need to increase the amount they send, either they increase the countries they sent it to, or increase the sales figures for some countries, or they expand the operation. First the magazine went international, then Literary Services, then Newsletters, then Publishing. Now it's Writing Workshops and Correspondence Courses."

"Where do you get this information?" Martinez said. "What do you do when I'm not around?"

"Write for magazines," I said. "Believe it or not, I did a how-to article on tourist use of black markets a few years ago. Lu—"

"What about the people?" Martinez asked. "You'd need to bring more people into it."

"One per country," I said. "And you can check up on them. How many times did Michael go to Greece in the past two years?"

"Six times to Greece," he admitted. "Three times to Italy. Once to Spain."

"Until Alida cut him off," I said. I paused. It was like looking at a nonrepresentational painting. If you held it one way, then started to turn it around, you got—differences. Sometimes you got a whole different picture. "You know," I said, "when I first thought of this, I thought they were all in on it. But if Alida *wasn't* in on it, then it would explain the murders."

"If Alida wasn't in on it," Martinez said, "nobody was making any money. Except the company, and why would the rest of them do it to just make money for the company?"

"Felicity Aldershot was making money," I said. "She has an employment contract that guarantees her a percentage of the profits from any expansion she initiates. It was her idea to go international in the first place. All she has to do is rig the laundering so her bonuses equal her shipments, then she can pass the money out to the others. She can pass money to Michael and Jack, anyway. She passes dope to Stephen."

"This explains the murders?" Martinez said.

"Of course it does," I said. "Alida cut Michael off. Let's assume this was all Felicity's idea. She's got the brains to figure this out. So does Stephen, but he doesn't have the drive. Anyway, she picks up most of the income and the others get less, but still a hefty monthly addition to the ridiculous salaries Alida paid them. Maybe Alida had a point. Even when they got money they couldn't hang on to it. Anyway, Michael was still spending more than he was bringing in, so he started embezzling and Alida found out about it. The others got nervous. The last thing they wanted was Alida figuring it out and booting them or taking a cut or whatever, so they cut him off, too. To punish him. And Michael started getting crazy. He rigged that thing up in the wardrobe so he could see how many magazines were going out. How many would tell him how much money was coming in, the two things would have to be tied. But punishing wasn't working. He kept getting crazier. That peephole was crazy behavior. One of them found out about Ivy Samuels Tree and the contract— Phoebe said it's more or less common knowledge in the business —and wrote a half-innocuous letter to her. They probably told Michael it was for real. He was supposed to play the great crusader and protest against the injustice done her. From what I've heard about Michael he would have liked that. Then when Ivy came one of them called Michael on the interoffice phone and told him something that scared him—scared him enough to make him head for that wardrobe. He got Ivy out of his office and went to look and they killed him."

"You keep saying 'they'."

"It could have been any of them," I said. "Felicity sent Janet away from her desk and took Ivy in to Michael, but as far as I can tell, it would have been better to leave Janet at her desk. Wait.

No. You don't want Janet to see Ivy leave. You couldn't count on her not seeing Michael after that."

"It was Felicity Aldershot?"

"Can't tell," I said. "Could have been. Could have been Jack. Could have been collusion. Anyway, then the police decided to attach the records and they got worried Alida would find out about it anyway. So they killed Alida. All it took was a call to Ivy. Then Mrs. Haskell—you see, it wasn't the audit. It was the attachment. They didn't want some smart lawyer looking through the records of what went where and why. With the police in and out they probably didn't have time to fix whatever they needed to fix. So they had to put Mrs. Haskell out of commission for a while. They didn't have to kill her. They didn't kill her."

"No," Martinez said, "they didn't kill her. She's still in a coma, but she's looking up. Last I heard, anyway."

"See," I said. "The attack on Mrs. Haskell makes me think it's Jack. It's the kind of thing Jack would do. He gets emotional. The other two aren't emotional. I think one of them did it and the other two don't necessarily know who it was. That's why everybody over there seems like they're on an amphetamine high. That's why Jack—Jesus Christ," I said. "*Jack.*"

"Jack *what?*" Martinez said.

"Jack's going to commit suicide," I said.

THIRTY-SIX

Martinez stopped to pay the bill. He got out of the Park Luncheonette a full minute after I did. I didn't stop for anything. I didn't button my coat or wind my scarves around my throat. I stuffed my gloves in my pockets. My hands were once again smeared with black. I didn't bother trying to rub them off. I didn't have time.

"Jack Brookfield's going to commit suicide," Martinez said, catching up with me. "Are you crazy? Even if he murdered those people, we've got Ivy, we can't get rid of Ivy without proof, we haven't got proof. I don't care how good your theories are. We haven't got *proof*."

"They're going to make him commit suicide," I said. "The gloves. That's what happened to the gloves."

"McKenna—"

"I left my gloves in his office. On the radiator. He had a lot of pairs of gloves, over a dozen, all black. They looked almost exactly like mine. Hell, as long as they were black and on that radiator, I don't think it would have made any difference, not if whoever it was was in a hurry."

"In a hurry to do what?"

"To put typewriter ink on the gloves," I said. "Jack went out to lunch. He and Felicity went out at the same time but I don't know if they had lunch together. Stephen was wandering around the office by himself. It couldn't have been Marty Lahler because he was helping me with the wardrobe."

"Who's Marty Lahler? How does he come into this?"

"The accountant," I said. "Queens. Forget it. It's a long story. It had to be while Jack was out, though, and they wouldn't know how long he'd be out, so they'd be in a hurry. They came in and grabbed a pair of gloves and put typewriter ink on them. Just in case."

"Just in case *what?*"

"Just in case being half a million dollars in the hole and in violation of the securities laws wasn't enough to make his death look like a suicide."

We reached the door to the Writing Enterprises building. I pushed it back so hard it knocked against the concession stand and made the candy jump. The single working elevator was on the eighth floor. I pushed frantically at the button. Then I leaned against it. The elevators were the old-fashioned kind. When you pressed the call button, bells rang in any car off the call floor. They sounded like burglar alarms.

"That man I heard in Jack's office today," I said. "He was talking about them ending up in Leavenworth. Jack's been speculating in securities and he's in a hole and he's in a big enough hole his broker thinks they're both going to go down and that means an SEC investigation and that means—"

"I see what it means."

The elevator started gliding downward.

"They can't have this kind of trouble," I said. "Not so it touches them. If Jack panics and kills himself, it won't touch them. Nobody will press it."

"How're they going to get him to kill himself?"

"Writing Enterprises," I said, "is twenty stories up."

Martinez said, "Jesus Christ," for what felt like the millionth time.

The elevator hit the lobby and let out an irate fat woman in purple tweeds.

The elevator that gets you to work in the morning goes much too fast, unless you're late. When you're late, it hardly seems to move at all. This was one of those elevators that hardly moved at all. I swear to God it took the better part of two hours to get to the twentieth floor.

We stopped on every floor in between. Every time we stopped someone got in, said "Oh, you're going *up*," and got out again. "Look at the arrow," I said, the third time it happened. "Look at the *arrow*. It's *green*. It points *up*."

Martinez tried to calm me down. He told me it was all conjecture. He told me that even if my conjecture was accurate, nothing said they had to force Jack to suicide *tonight*.

"Of course it has to be tonight," I said. "That Dunne person was in the office today. The further they get away from that the less plausible the suicide is."

"Felicity Aldershot or Stephen Brookfield," Martinez said.

"I'll bet on Felicity Aldershot," I said. "That bitch."

"Now, now," Martinez said.

"Can't they make this elevator go faster?" I said.

"What do you want? Four on the floor?"

We got to the twentieth floor. The elevator doors opened. We couldn't get out.

The entire reception area of Writing Enterprises was full of people. Pink tissue paper hearts hung from the ceiling. Pink tissue paper streamers were tacked to the walls. A mouse-faced editorial assistant peered at Martinez and me and said drunkenly, "People in the elevator! Look! People in the elevator!"

"Keep your head down," Martinez said. "Act like they aren't there."

He put his hands on my shoulders and pushed. I went flying into the crowd, bumping against heads and shoulders and knees. A few people swore at me. Most of them laughed. I came up short at the desk and found myself looking down at a huge crystal punch bowl full of something green. Someone I didn't recognize filled a paper cup with the green and handed it to me.

"Should have been pink," she said. "Got drunk on the way to Woolworth's. Got it mixed up with Saint Patrick's Day."

"Right," I said.

"Which way?" Martinez said.

I pointed through the mass of people to the corridor.

"His office," I said. "That would be the logical place. His office."

"Come on." Martinez grabbed my arm and started dragging me through the people, using me as a shield to keep them from crowding in behind him. The corridor wasn't much better than the reception area. It had become a public lover's lane. Pairs of every possible description were lined up against the wall, locked together in a kind of rigor coitus.

"You'd think sex was complicated *enough*," Martinez said. "People have to make it more complicated. People have to get fancy."

We got to the first office corridor and ran down it, glad of the air and the space. We turned the corner and came to Jack Brook-field's office. Martinez stopped dead in front of the door.

"If I was in the hole for half a million dollars," he said, "I'd jump out a window myself."

"What's that supposed to mean?" I asked him.

"It means maybe they're making him commit suicide and maybe they're not, but one thing is for sure. He's got a good reason to put himself out a window. If he *is* putting himself out a window, without help, then the last thing we want to do is bust in on him."

"Jesus Christ," I said. "What brought that up?"

"Listen," Martinez said. "You won't hear anything."

I listened. No sound at all came from Jack Brookfield's office.

"Maybe it's over," I said. "Maybe they've done it already."

"There'd have been some reaction by now," Martinez said. "It took us long enough to get up in that elevator."

"Maybe not," I said.

"Trust me."

I tried the doorknob. It turned easily. I pushed the door in on darkness. I felt along the wall and hit the light switch.

Jack Brookfield's office was empty. The windows were closed. The desk was clear. Martinez let out enough air to power a wind-mill for a month.

"Damn," he said. "Damn. All for nothing. Crap."

"No," I said. "Listen."

Martinez wanted to believe I'd invented the whole thing, but he couldn't help hearing the sound I heard. Someone was tap-ping against glass.

I went back into the first main corridor and listened. The tapping was louder. A voice said, "Stop." The tapping stopped.

Martinez pointed to a door. "In there," he said.

"It doesn't make sense," I told him.

He shrugged. "Sense or no sense. In there. Get around the corner and stay out of sight. I don't want you anywhere near this."

This was more arrogance than I could handle in one day. Especially that day. I wasn't going to take it like a girl. I brushed past Martinez, said, "Crap," in my loudest voice, and kicked in the door.

It was a good thing I did. When that door swung open, Stephen Brookfield was halfway out his office window. Standing right behind him, holding a gun to his back, was Jack.

There was an explanation, of course. There always is. I didn't get it for a while. Instead of doing what everybody expected him to do—drop the gun and run—Jack headed straight for Stephen and pushed. If he'd been a second faster, he'd have got what he wanted, though what he expected to gain from it was beyond me. Stephen, seeing us, had pulled just a fraction of an inch back into the room. It was enough to let him keep his balance when Jack came hurtling at him. Jack bounced off him and hit the floor. Then Martinez went to work.

Martinez is very good at what he does. He got the gun away from Jack with only one shot fired. The one shot went into Stephen Brookfield's desk, shattering a desk leg. The desk buckled, teetered, and fell over. Stephen said, "Good riddance," and started to laugh. Martinez motioned me to the phone. I called the cops. While I was calling, the party wandered into the corridor and to the edge of the door, bringing punch. It was very good punch, .0001 percent green food coloring and 99.9999 percent straight vodka. Even Stephen took some. He raised his glass to me in a toast and said,

"Felicity's going to kill him. This is the fourth one he's screwed up."

THIRTY-SEVEN

"She would have killed him," I told Martinez, when the uniformed police had taken their positions and the crowd had been dispersed and Jack Brookfield was safely in custody. "I would say she would have killed him 'too,' except she hasn't actually killed anyone yet."

"Jack did it all?" Martinez said.

"Yeah," I said. "Jack did it all."

I reached for my cigarettes and found an empty pack. Stephen got out a pack of his own—Trues—and tossed them over to me. He'd disappeared into the bathroom some time ago and emerged very calm. He was still very calm. The idea of all those policemen and all that dope in the same place at the same time didn't bother him at all.

"Everybody thought Alida was nuts," Stephen said. "Alida wasn't nuts. Felicity was nuts. Alida didn't trust us and she was right."

"Alida trusted Felicity," I said.

"We all make mistakes," Stephen said.

"Will somebody tell me what's going on?" Martinez said.

Stephen patted my arm. "You've got to watch him," he said, pointing to Martinez. "If you don't give him what he wants, he can lock you up. Or harass you. Or—"

"Or tell her boyfriend what she's been up to," Martinez said. "That ought to make me an accessory before the fact in a homicide case."

"Oh, shit," I said. "I called him. I called Nick. He'll be here in fifteen minutes."

"Tell me," Martinez said. "Then I won't tell him. Much."

Stephen and I were stretched out on the carpet, our backs against the pasteboard wall. We were side to side, shoulder to shoulder. He reached out and patted my knee.

"Miss McKenna was ahead of herself," Stephen said. "Felicity had to get rid of Jack because Jack had not only killed two people and battered a third, he knew he'd done it because she asked him to. Told him to, more likely. She found out about Ivy Samuels Tree—I remember when she told us about that. She didn't tell us what she was going to do about it, but she told us. She thought up the typewriter ribbons. She—"

"I thought you didn't know any of this," Martinez said. "I thought you weren't in on it."

"I wasn't," Stephen said. "I'm not an idiot, Lieutenant. Jack was an idiot. Michael came close. Felicity was smart enough to be sure she couldn't be caught for any of this, though I didn't know she was using Jack until he tried to force me out a window. And I *know* he screwed them up. Felicity would have been smart enough to know one murder in the office was enough, and that should be done as unexceptionally as possible. Not in a wardrobe in a newly cleaned out broom closet. And then the money—"

"The money?" Martinez said.

"The money in Alida's purse," Stephen said. "Jack went in and took it after Miss McKenna here found the body. He asked me for five dollars that morning, and that afternoon he had enough to take himself out to MacArthur Park for a serious lunch. Felicity sure as hell wasn't going to give it to him, no matter what he'd just done for her. Felicity can hang on to a dollar better than the Internal Revenue Service. And then you started asking about the position of the chair, and the money in the wallet, and Felicity started looking like she'd swallowed a worm. Like I said, stupidity was never my problem."

"Except in one area," I said.

He gave me a look that said, "Skip it." "She had to get rid of me before she got rid of Jack," he said, "because I kept going around doing things. I accidentally left a certain article in a book I gave Miss McKenna—"

"Just McKenna," I said. "Or Pay."

"Patience?"

"Never Patience," I said.

"Anyway, I left a certain article in this book," Stephen said. "Then when she came to give it back, I gave her hints. The hints were overheard. Miss McKenna and I were in the—ah, yes, the men's room." Stephen smiled at the look on Martinez's face. Martinez thought this was a bit much, even for me. "Felicity was in the ladies' room next door. The walls around here are paper."

"Marty Lahler said she'd gone out to lunch," I said.

"She did. Just after. She took Jack with her and had a nice long talk."

"What about the ink on McKenna's gloves?" Martinez said. "We had that all worked out as being a way for making Jack look like the killer. In case suicide because of financial ruin didn't work. Except Jack was the killer."

"If you go through the gloves on his radiator, you'll probably find a pair with ink dried on them," Stephen said. "Maybe two pair. Jack never could keep his gloves straight. He used Miss McKenna's gloves to ink up my raincoat. Just in case, as Patience would say."

"Don't call me Patience," I said.

Tony Marsh stuck his head in the door and said, "They picked her up. She was at home. Watching a videotape of *Gone With the Wind*."

"*Gone With the Wind*," Martinez said. "Jesus Christ."

"Says she doesn't know anything," Tony Marsh said.

"Tell her we took Jack Brookfield alive," Martinez said. "That ought to change her story."

"That'll end her story," Stephen said. "She won't say a word until her lawyer gets there."

"Doesn't matter," Martinez said.

"She has a very good lawyer," Stephen said.

Martinez shrugged. "This time, Jack Brookfield being Jack Brookfield, I don't think I care."

"Jack Brookfield being Jack Brookfield," Stephen agreed. "You know, he should have known. As long as Alida was alive, Felicity needed us to cover for her. With Alida gone, Felicity was in charge. She not only didn't need us, she couldn't afford to keep us around. All Jack could think about was the money he owed Tommy Dunne and what people would think of him if there was an SEC investigation. All Jack could ever think about was what people would think of him."

"So he killed two people, bashed up a third, and tried to force you out a window at gunpoint?" Martinez said.

"He cared what Felicity thought of him," Stephen said. "He wanted Felicity to think he was a big tough man."

"I don't believe it," Martinez said.

"I don't believe it either," I said. "It's easier to say he was afraid to say no to her. He was afraid to say no to anybody. He hated having people mad at him."

"This is the screwiest thing I've ever heard," Martinez said.

Tony Marsh stuck his head back into the office, looking sheepish.

"The other one's out here," he said. "The short one. She's got —ah—dinner."

Phoebe's voice floated in from the corridor. "I've got enough food for everybody," she said. "I've even got enough plates. I've got plastic forks. You have to let me through."

"Let her through," Nick said. "This stuff is heavy. And it's *hot.*"

EPILOGUE

Murder, as I said, is only the beginning. As soon as I saw the *Post* edition with LOVE GIRL LICKS ANOTHER ONE for a headline, I knew I didn't want to stick around for the encores. I made my statements to the police and went over my probable testimony with the district attorney's office. I left an address with Martinez and took the first plane I could get to London. Nick got the cat and a note. "I don't care what kind of principles you've got," I told him. "Either get this relationship moving or get out of it."

I stayed in London nine months. During those nine months, the following things happened:

Irene Haskell recovered. Phoebe got a copy of her manuscript, read it, did some minor corrections, and sent it to a friend of hers at Harlequin. Irene ended up with a contract for four books and the pen name Irina Hayes. She still wanted to sue Writing Enterprises, even though there wasn't much of it left. The fact that her book had been accepted for publication so easily and with so little revision *proved* they'd been conning her.

Ivy Samuels Tree recovered, too, although it took longer. Nick used the publicity she got from the Brookfield murders—all good, after the papers could portray her as a helpless (and beautiful) victim—to pressure Dortman and Hodges into putting her own picture on the back of her books. He even got them to sponsor a publicity tour for her latest, *Castle on the Moors*. *Castle on the Moors* was due out in January. With any luck, by that time Ivy would have stopped talking about sleepwalking altogether.

Janet Grasky got a job typing for Joan Liddell, was promoted to general secretary, and started night classes at Brooklyn College toward a bachelor's degree in business. Joan was paying for

Brooklyn College. She had also given Janet a raise. Janet, released from the defeating atmosphere of Writing Enterprises, had got religion. She believed in ambition, efficiency, and the sanctity of hard cash the way a devout Catholic believes in papal infallibility.

Writing Enterprises closed. Martin Lahler went first to a company making plastic frogs that swam in bathtubs and phosphorescent bumper stickers with sexy logos—as sexy was defined in 1948. They went bankrupt thirteen weeks after he arrived. He then moved to a company making whoopee cushions, exploding cigars, and ties that squirt water. He should be happy there. They've been going bankrupt for years.

Stephen Brookfield was not arrested for possession of heroin, or anything else. He was the district attorney's favorite witness. He had to be taken care of. They arranged a protracted stay at a very expensive, very elegant drug treatment center upstate. He sent me a postcard from there. "This is impossible," he said. "I seem to be doing it anyway."

Phoebe sent me an entire letter. I quote: "I had Nick here last night with his new law partner who is David Grossman and knows my mother's sister's husband from Green Haven which is to say the rich side of the family and I told him about my parents and Union City and he didn't seem upset. He's very dedicated. I admire people who are very dedicated even if they don't eat enough and he doesn't seem to mind that I eat too much and he reads all my books and is very impressed and we are going to Mamma Leone's Thursday and get a table big enough for just the two of us. He says maybe we should go to a concert first because there's the Amati Quartet at Lincoln Center and I think if we do that it will be a Real Date. What do you think?" I think Phoebe is in love. It ought to be interesting. I have never seen Phoebe in love. I have never seen Phoebe with enough time for any love other than the kind that can be put into the pages of a romance novel. I also think David Grossman would do well to be a nice man. If he isn't, both Nick and I will kill him. Sequentially. It is a fallacy that you can only die once.

Nobody wrote me about the case. They didn't have to. I got

The International Herald Tribune. The International Herald Tribune is hardly the New York *Post*, but it did manage to give me the essential information. It reported Jack Brookfield's guilty plea, for instance. It also reported Felicity Aldershot's suicide. Having been released on bail through the prolonged and overpaid efforts of an internationally famous murder defense specialist, she went home, stuck the barrel of a Saturday night special in her mouth, and blew off the back of her head.

I waited for the publicity to die down. Then, on a cold day in early December, I caught a plane for New York.

Nick met me at JFK. He took my bags, got us a cab, and asked how I enjoyed my flight. He knows how I enjoy flights. I don't enjoy flights. The only way I could enjoy a flight is if I were unconscious.

When we were crossing the Fifty-ninth Street Bridge, he asked me, "Are you jet-lagged? I've got something to tell you I don't want to tell you unless you're jet-lagged."

"What if I'm not jet-lagged?" I asked him. "You never tell me?"

"I wait till you're drunk," he said.

"I'm jet-lagged," I said. "I'm also hung over, because I drank too much so I wouldn't be scared. I'm also exhausted because I can never sleep on planes and I can never sleep the night before I have to ride on a plane."

He considered this and found it good. He knew me. He said, "All right. Get ready. This is it. *I can't stand not having you around.*"

I put my cigarette in the half-inch-wide ashtray on the cab door and turned to him. He does look like Christopher Reeve. And he means well.

"All right," I said. "I can't stand not having you around, either."

"I *don't* like casual shit," he said. "Casual has nothing to do with a relationship. A relationship is never casual no matter what you think."

"Give it up," I told him. "I won't sleep with anybody else but you as long as I'm sleeping with you. That far I'll go. Any farther I won't go."

"That far you'll go?" Nick said.

"That far I'd always have gone," I said.

"Shit," he said. "Two years I've been arguing this one. Two *years.*"

I said something unintelligibly soothing, put out my cigarette, and laid my head in his lap. I'd had the day. I closed my eyes and didn't open them again until Nick started bouncing around on the seat, looking through his pockets for money to give the driver.